I0782154

OVERBOARD

OVERBOARD

S.C. MEGALE

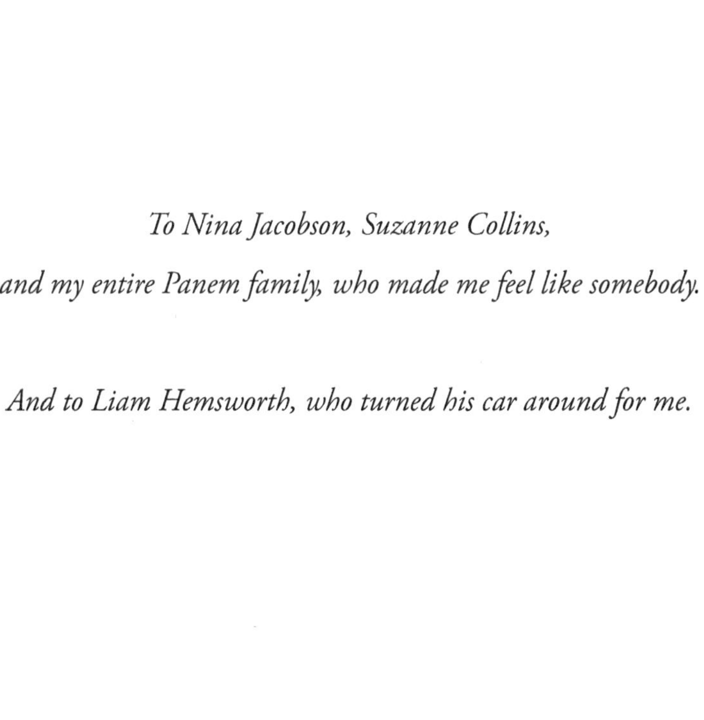

To Nina Jacobson, Suzanne Collins,

and my entire Panem family, who made me feel like somebody.

And to Liam Hemsworth, who turned his car around for me.

PART ONE:

SURFACE

ONE

Bubbles streamed from Markham's mouth. A strong current flushed him dozens of feet underwater, and all he saw was turquoise and blue and white. Then his shoulder banged into something hard. And again—like a pinball springing back and forth. Just as Markham's lungs began to burn, a surge of water burped him up and into the . . .

Surface.

Froth leapt around him like in a hot tub. He gasped. Like planks of wood, other fish burst to the surface of the tank: strange, flat-as-pancakes fish; fish with bodies riddled like chain link fences; purple ones; red ones; one the size of a large pig. They flapped their gills, mouths open and eyes blank.

Over the rim of the tank and through salt-stung eyes Markham saw the copper gleam of pots and pans lining shelves, heard the scrape and clank of kitchenware at work. Steam furled into the air, and he caught glimpses of white-clad shoulders and tall hats walking between countertops.

He pressed his palm to the glass before him. Yes. He was in a tank.

Hands plunged into the water next to him and hauled out two yellow-and-orange fish that slapped each other with such ferocity droplets sprang into Markham's eyes. On the other side, different hands dove down, and then more, all pulling out the harvested seafood.

A strong hand grabbed him.

Exclamations of alarm resounded from the cooks as Markham seemed to birth from the water, huge and heavy and human. He flopped down on the floor, and the cooks stepped back. Foam from the tank bubbled over onto his head as he clawed himself into a sitting position.

The culinarians chattered and moved their hands in argument, their language overlapping so much it was impossible to tell whether or not they spoke in one tongue. Behind them, others in the kitchen continued their work as normal: Cooks jumped back as flames pounced into the air. Trellises of grease hissed. Rows of lids teetered on boiling pots. Several running sinks seethed to join the symphony.

But Markham's mouth snapped closed on sight of the monster.

Halfway across the kitchen, it stood on two legs, its claws clasped behind its back. A Jurassic tail crept from its puffy grey chef pants, and it wore a white double-breasted coat. A chef hat perched atop its scaly green head. The reptilian chef listened intently to a human showing it what appeared to be a laminated menu.

And then the crocodile heard the commotion and turned its head towards Markham.

Markham's heart stopped.

Its reptilian eyes held him, black as beads. Without unclasping its claws behind its back, it moved slowly towards Markham with smooth, long strides.

The other kitchen workers backed away at the mutant crocodile's approach out of either fear or respect. When the beast stopped in front of Markham, it stood over seven feet tall. It leaned down to get a better look. A dried, white sand dollar dangled from its neck in the air between them.

Markham shook as he gazed up into the face of the monster. A puff of hot air from its wide green snout blew down onto him and he breathed in the crocodile's scent, a musty jasmine like the inside of an antique jewelry box.

Slowly, the crocodile clamped down on either side of Markham's shoulders with its claws. Markham squeezed his eyes closed in terror, assuming this was his last moment. In one fluid motion, the crocodile lifted him to his feet with firm, effortless strength.

Markham opened his eyes.

The monster was still, in the way only a reptile could be, but its pupilless eyes darted back and forth over him with unnerving humanity and calculation, and Markham felt already eaten, already pumped through its stomach, already stolen into the reptile's being.

And then the crocodile, still bracing Markham on either shoulder, dropped its jaw in what could only be interpreted as a grin. Its eyes were somehow bright.

Just as the beast began to raise one claw to its chef hat— for what reason Markham didn't know—another, darker claw snatched the chef's claw down. Markham jumped.

Nearly a foot taller stood what must have been the reptile's sibling/cousin/twisted uncle. It grasped the green crocodile's shoulders with both claws and glared at Markham from over the shoulder of its kin, eyes vertical slits unlike the chef's, and kindling fire somehow. Its brown scales were chafed in a maze of scars, like a snake caught in mid-molt. Unlike the chef crocodile, it wore a black leather vest and no hat or pants. Another sand dollar pendant dangled from its neck, but this one was snapped in half and painted black.

Affronted, the green crocodile turned its long snout towards the other, and they communicated in strange, guttural noises, neck muscles bobbing. The brown one's dinosaur-like claw tightened around its kin's, and it shifted a reproachful gaze on the green one as if in warning. And then, with one more glare at Markham, the brown crocodile dropped to its belly and streaked away, zigzagging with lightning speed up the wall and into an open vent, its tail swishing once before disappearing.

Markham's breath hitched in his chest and did not release.

Slowly the crocodile chef turned its eyes back to Markham. It gulped as if to apologize. After one more glance at the vent, the green crocodile relaxed, opening its jaw joyfully once more, although a little less wide. It lifted a claw and waved Markham farther into the kitchen.

All the human cooks . . . did they not mind? Was this normal? They looked up from chopping mountains of curly, lavender-colored stalks at cutting boards and watched Markham pass. But they were unperturbed by the crocodile pair. Markham dragged his gaze over them almost pleadingly, but, finding no response, followed the beast.

Tiny claws thumped the top of a silver table to his left, and scaly feet wagged beneath the surface. Two baby crocodiles squeaked at his passing with excitement, jaws open and full of pearly little pin-prick teeth. But their smiles didn't seem to be in the jovial fashion of the master chef.

One pointed at Markham with its fork.

The back of the chef's claw whacked over the little crocodile. The babies scrambled over their seats, growling and chirping deep in their throats, but the adult crocodile branded them with a scolding look, a frown cutting down its jagged mouth.

The master chef stopped at a human apprentice and gestured to Markham and then to a far door with a porthole window, grunting things in reptilian. The human apprentice nodded.

"Yes, Master Gavial. I'll fetch her immediately." He placed down a set of knives and moved for the door.

"Fetch–?" began Markham, but it was futile. Master Gavial only turned a rolling eye to him. But his—no longer "its"–silence was benevolent. Markham's fear around the reptile subsided.

The apprentice returned through the metal swinging door, a woman in his wake.

Slender and dark-haired, her smooth, tight skin shone with luster and exertion, a single delicate dark freckle on her shoulder. No more than twenty-one. Sparsely-beaded pearl necklace around her neck. It held a sand dollar amulet like all the others wore, but hers was younger, olive green still, with the texture of fuzz still clinging to its paling edges. Markham picked up every detail—a servers' apron wrapped around her waist, and she held her head high, not in pride but defense, scanning the entire kitchen, familiar but wary.

Her hazel eyes met Markham's, and he felt his breath slip like an ice cube his throat tried to catch. But she tore her gaze away quickly and looked at Master Gavial.

"*How* did this–?"

Master Gavial said something in chirps and grunts, indicating the door again.

The young woman blinked. And then she shook her head and moved over to Markham.

"Come on," she said.

He glanced at her left hand as it grasped the soaking clothes on his shoulder. She was missing her ring finger. Her words were breathy and filled with true trepidation, only loud enough for his ear.

"You have no idea what you're in for."

TWO

"I know you didn't come from the tank."

Her voice was matter-of-fact. Markham allowed her to tighten the sash of the dark green robe she had changed him into. It was warm and dry.

"I didn't," he said. "I ended up in the tank."

The young woman scoffed. She turned to where the towels lay folded and crisp on a shelf. Tens of tiny little black frogs sat on the towels and watched with fascinated, wide yellow eyes. Innocent, but nosy.

"Get out of here!" she shooed, and they all hopped off with *ribbits*, slapping onto the floor and tumbling away like a giant cartwheel. "I *hate* them." She grabbed a towel, no trace of humor in her voice.

"Here." The woman shoved the towel into Markham's hands.

His gaze was still in the direction of the disappearing frogs. "Dry your hair."

He lifted a hand to his hair. The woman's eyes lingered on its silver color, and he caught the glance, watching her reaction with a tint of hopefulness.

"How old are you?" she said.

"Twenty-six." He dipped his head and ruffled the towel into his hair.

"Did you have a stressful life?"

"I told you." His words were muffled. "I can't remember my life."

Markham handed her back the towel, hair tousled but dry. She continued to gaze at him curiously.

"You've come to the right place, then," she said, almost carefully. "I've been here my whole life, and yet sometimes I forget, too."

"What's your name?" Markham asked as if he couldn't wait any longer.

She paused. "My name is Nina."

"Nina." He had to say it.

"Yeah…" She glanced at him. It had been a little weird.

Markham cleared his throat. "And that's . . ." He looked through the porthole into the giant kitchen again. "Master Gavial?"

A human cook presented a plate of fish to Master Gavial, who looked down at it for a long beat, claws clasped behind his back. Then Gavial snapped the food into his jaws and flipped back his head, pumping the fish down his throat. Markham recoiled, but then Gavial braced the cook on either shoulder as he had done to Markham and dropped his jaw approvingly. The human cook smiled.

"Yeah," said Nina. "He's the kitchen master."

"You could understand him," said Markham.

"After a while you pick up some nuances."

They both paused as they observed through the window.

"Look," said Nina. "We should probably–"

"What about the brown crocodile?"

Silence. Nina fiddled with the stub of her missing finger in either annoyance or . . . wariness. The peculiar manner pulled Markham's eyes to her.

"That's his cousin. His name is Crocidius."

Markham stared at her–in a socially acceptable way this time.

Still this aggravated Nina, who tugged off her apron and flung it into the laundry bin next to the towels, turning away. "Yes, they're both cleverly reptilian names."

"That's not why I was staring at you."

"I'm beginning to gather that."

Blood coursed to Markham's face.

"I mean *who* are they? *How are they* –?"

"Look." Nina spun back to him. "I don't know how you got here, but you're about to see a lot of things on this ship that don't make sense. If I were you, I'd start pretending that they made perfect sense. Otherwise you can jump overboard and the Captain won't turn us around and save you. Make sense?"

Markham froze. It made no sense. But in accordance with what she had just instructed . . .

He nodded.

"Good. He wants me to feed you now. Then you're pretty much on your own."

"You called this a ship."

Nina began to move out of the laundry room and farther from the kitchen. Markham kept pace, speaking all the while.

"You called this a ship. Is that what I'm on? A ship?"

"You'd never know it, but yes. I guess the fishing pipes pulled you in from underwater."

Markham dropped his eyes to the floor, where they followed the path of small inky frog prints.

"Are we following—?"

"They'll go towards the food. No more questions."

Nina pushed open a pair of heavy, red-cushioned doors and led them into a sprawling dining room.

A chandelier the size of a small moon hung from wires in the center of the atrium. Its thousands of crystals sparkled out rainbows. Below, a sea of round, clothed tables held spherical candleholders that pulsed with light. Servers trailed between the tables, holding aloft covered dishes while silverware clinked. In the dim light, Markham couldn't see much more than shadows on the faces of the diners, but he noticed one of them dabbing a napkin to her mouth with what looked like a paw. Two humans laughed and chinked together glasses full of a black drink bubbling with seaweed and pineapple.

Nina grasped Markham's wrist and towed him to a seat.

He spread the cloth napkin over his lap and watched different trays of meals pass. Despite the oddity of the foods, their aroma was alluring, drawing saliva to his mouth.

Above the dining room, level with the chandelier, another floor rung around the walls, its open rails looking down onto the eaters. Since the chandelier was suspended by wires (miles of it, it seemed), Markham could look right past the crystals above him and see unending ceiling, more and more stories going up and disappearing into darkness. Somewhere far up in the blackness was a glow of light blue—and by the way it got brighter or dimmer traveling up and down floors, respectively, Markham realized it was a giant glass elevator taking up the entire space of the atrium. Shadowy figures trailed around the many balconied stories up above, but that was the most detail he could make out.

Markham swallowed and pulled his eyes down, focusing again on Nina, who sat across from him.

"Am I all right to sit here in a green robe?" There didn't seem to be a formal dress code.

"That counts as a question," said Nina.

"I don't think I can speak for the next few days in anything but questions." Markham ran his fingers along the tablecloth and focused on the rush of smooth, cool material to soothe his nerves. *How could all these humans . . . how are they all not aghast, not with bandages around their scalps?*

"Then you won't speak. Even better." Ice tickled Nina's lip as she took a drink from the complimentary water, looking at him over the rim.

"Do I have to—?" Nope. That was a question. Markham cleared his throat. "I should order from a menu."

"No, you shouldn't," Nina said. "Just wait."

Sure enough, dishes were placed down at random on their table from the rotating servers. All Master Gavial's doing, no doubt. Alongside one plate, a server also dropped a sizzling skillet, lined not with food but hot spatulas. Nina selected a spatula without preamble and lifted the cover off her dish.

Insects hopped out like a fountain. She whacked them with the spatula, and one after one burnt instantly.

"O-Okay that is horrifying." Markham's hand clamped firmly over the cover to his own dish.

Nina popped an insect in her mouth. "They're better fresh."

Markham stooped down and tilted the lid off his dish just a crack to peek inside. No bugs flooded out.

"How old are you again? Twenty-six? The bugs don't live more than a day anyway, Twenty-Six. We're not *monsters*."

"Gavial has some pretty advanced breeding techniques in that kitchen, huh."

To Markham's surprise, Nina actually gave a snort.

"What's you finding what's funny, toots?" A large, bare stomach bumped into the back of Nina's chair. The new voice was low as a bullfrog's.

Nina's laugh cut short. Markham straightened at the table, gripping its rim with both hands. Nina's shoulders squared, and she slowly set down her spatula. Behind her were two humanoids, seven feet tall and round as bowling balls. They dressed like pirates with ugly, sparkly bandanas around their necks and shirts four sizes too small. Each had a *K* embroidered into their shirt sleeve. Strangely, the tops of their heads were plateaued—an opening, maybe?—and smoke curled out and draped like hair around them.

"Weren't you two given restraining orders from the kitchen?" Nina retorted. Her voice was flat and unperturbed, but her body language didn't reflect this. She kept her eyes on the table, holding the top of her water glass and tipping it back and forth with her four-fingered hand.

The gangster leaned down into her personal space and laid a greasy hand over her four-fingered one to stop its movement.

"Kloff's is getting *impatient*."

Markham could smell the foulness of his breath from across the table—it was like burnt paper. Nina closed her eyes. But when the gangster's other hand crept into Nina's hair and twirled it . . .

"*Hey!*" Markham barked. Then fear reprimanded him. Heat flushed his face, but it was too late to back out now. "Pick on someone your own size." He set his jaw.

The gangsters raised their eyes to him.

Plates shook on the table as the first gangster moved over to Markham. He stooped down into Markham's face.

"Would that be you?"

The stench almost did him in. But Markham replied.

"Would I have to wear that bandana?"

From the corner of his eye, Markham saw Nina give a—*was it possible?*—meek, timid smile.

The gangster boomed with laughter, holding his stomach with both hands and leaning back. "Where's this guy, where from?"

"He's not from here, he's, nope!" chortled the other enormous gangster in a voice so high it was almost comical.

The first gangster slapped Markham on the back and trundled away, pointing a meaty finger at Nina.

"Kloff's is impatient!"

"Do you even know what apostrophes are for?" said Markham, heated from the slap.

They meandered off, having to walk sideways to fit between the tables. Markham watched them over Nina's shoulder for a good minute before looking at her.

"Notice he didn't answer."

Again, Nina's eyes were down, but she gave a shy smile.

"What's wrong?" Markham pressed. "What was that about?"

"You eat whatever's on your plate for five minutes and I'll explain as much as I can in that time and then we're going over there."

"Over where?"

"Over there." Nina didn't point. Didn't raise her head. Only darted her eyes over Markham's shoulder. He twisted in his chair, seeing past several more tables to a faculty door.

"Uh . . ."

"Eat."

He glanced down at the covered dish, gulping with trepidation. "Eat."

"All right, all right." He lifted the cover and sighed when he saw a harmless hunk of steak resting on thyme.

"We're on a ship," stated Nina.

"You 'ed that al'eady." Markham spoke through chewing.

"Well, you're going to forget. A lot. That's the point."

Markham swallowed. "Whose point? Some tyrannical navy?"

This time when Nina smiled, it was sad and real. "No, Twenty-Six. Look around."

He did. And he remembered his thoughts from only minutes ago: *Why didn't the humans care? Why weren't they afraid of insanity?*

"This isn't a ship to them. It's a city. A world. And it is. It never stops."

"Who's steering this ship?"

"The Captain."

"Who's that?"

"No one knows. He speaks to us through the First Mate some-times. The Captain is who gives us this life. They love him."

"They, not you?"

Nina went silent. It was not with attitude this time, but with contemplation—maybe even sadness. She fingered the fuzz of her green sand dollar necklace. Markham narrowed an eye as he studied it.

"I'm not so sure he's there," said Nina.

A pause. She looked up swiftly and continued as if those words were too poisonous to be left alone.

"But I hope he is. I think he's the only one who can help us now."

Markham cocked his head.

"Like what you just saw. The gangs and missing passengers and just . . . *bad* parts of the ship. You don't get it."

"The First Mate doesn't do anything on the Captain's behalf? Like . . . order around some police?"

"There used to be the Mariners to enforce the law. But Kloff killed or scared them all off. First Mate Yastley hasn't been very proactive lately—no one's seen him in months."

"So how does this ship even stay running if it never stops? Fuel and everything?"

"No one knows," said Nina.

"And where's the Captain steering it?"

"No one cares. It's been five minutes."

She pressed her legs hard against his beneath the table so abruptly he jumped, his chair scraping backward. His pulse hammered, and he lifted his gaze to her.

"Come on."

She got up and headed straight for the door without a second glance.

As soon as he entered, she closed the door and tugged him in with both hands.

"Wait, what–?"

She slammed her mouth against his. He stumbled forward and crashed his forearms against plastic crates of silverware, which shuffled and clinked at the impact.

They parted.

"God, woman." His voice was squeaky.

"Thank you for what you did back there. I don't want to see you again."

She kissed him hard again. A groan of near agony escaped his throat as she pulled back.

"God."

She placed her hand–her maimed one–gently over his face. His whole face. But strange as the gesture was, he didn't close his eyes; he continued to stare at her and pant between her four fingers.

"There's no god here, Twenty-Six. Only the Captain."

THREE

Nina disappeared after that, partly because the frogs arrived unannounced, and she stormed out of the room flinging a few off her shoulders. She pushed past Markham and fled for Gavial's kitchen. Markham didn't follow.

He staggered out of the faculty room.

With her gone, the reality of what he was seeing pounded in around him: Servers with extra sets of arms reaching across tables with exhausted, rosy-cheeked smiles. A giant brown ladybug sitting beneath one of the tables, looking like fallen food and then scurrying off dutifully a second later, others avoiding squishing it. Whether as a necklace, a bow, or a pin, sand dollars in every shade between white and green adorned each of them.

He slapped a hand over his eyes and then he ran. Knocked into tables and loped ahead like a football player. As bizarre as they were, most of the diners leaned back in their chairs to watch him with concern, exchanging mystified looks with one another.

Markham bowled up the staircase and broke into the first story hallway above the dining room. The darkness of the walls and dimly lit floors seemed like a safe harbor.

He rubbed the wristwatch on his left wrist.

So, I'm a watch guy? he thought. *Businessman who fell off a speedboat?*

He pounded a fist to his forehead.

What am I?!

What!

He leaned over and pressed his hands to his knees.

When ready, only then, he raised his eyes.

A neon blue sign glowed ahead. It was in the shape of an elevator. Markham shuffled towards it as if wounded, shoes skidding against the carpet like sandpaper. His hand swatted the elevator button and he leaned against the metal frame, counting to ten. Again. Again.

Above him a star of blue light descended, growing bigger the closer it got. The transparent lift growled as it slowed to a stop at the balcony. Markham stepped back in surprise. It was almost the size of the dining room itself, harboring midair like a spaceship. The doors rolled back to release other passengers, but they made no eye contact. One wore a dark plaid fedora and held a newspaper. Wires and microchips textured its hand. It dropped the newspaper in a trashcan near the balcony and walked towards the staircase.

Markham lunged for the paper and then dove between the closing elevator doors just in time.

"Okay," said Markham, flattening out the crinkled paper on

his ribs and leaning back onto the glass wall. He ignored the unmoving, black-cloaked figures that must have been homeless sitting in the corners of the elevator with wool blankets beneath them. Their jagged tin cans rattled as the lift groaned to make its ascent.

Markham squinted to read. Everything, the entire ship, seemed dark and shrouded. Maybe things were different during the daytime.

The front page announced in bold block letters:

Deck 58 Still Closed Due To Civil Unrest, All Crew Jobs Suspended

Beneath was a black-and-white photograph of a wall patched together with scrap metal and wood, closing off the entry into what must be the fifty-eighth deck.

Markham turned the page. He scanned down the columns. An article on new coral shipments at the jeweler's; a schedule of activities for the upcoming week, including Lionfish Club meetings at a "New location! Under Manhole 6!"; even a spiritual piece titled "Our Captain Sees."

And then, in the corner, what looked like a little-respected conspiracy article. "First Mate Missing? See Page 17."

Markham sandwiched the pages together and tore to the article as story after story blurred by. He remembered to glance at the rack of buttons near the elevator doors, which indicated a total of sixty floors. Above the buttons was a round, bronze naval seal, and below them, bars of red emergency buttons crusted with rust.

The lift slowed. It gave a burp this time and jiggled to a halt just as Markham found the first lines of the article. He moved for the exit subconsciously, not needing to see any more weird faces pass, only sensing the heat—or sometimes chill—of bodies traveling by.

He found a safe corner just past the elevator and read before going any farther. This is what Nina had been talking about.

Passengers! Isn't it time to wonder? A reliable source tells *The Blue Star News* that First Mate Charleston Yastley has not been seen by Mariners in nearly three months, the same amount of time since our Captain's last message. With followers growing anxious, awaiting a break to the Captain's silence on 58's shutdown, unaddressed crime, and missing passenger statistics rising, WHY would First Mate Yastley be so quiet? Is he the latest victim of gang kidnappings?

Someone bumped into Markham in passing and he looked up. Whatever floor this was, it was thrice as congested as the one he'd been on down below. Dinnertime must have been waning as nightlife emerged.

"None of this can be happening," Markham said at last. He tucked the paper under his arm and bolted away from the crowd.

He opened the first unlocked door he encountered, found a room conveniently full of pillows—no explanation offered—and collapsed.

Markham's demands that he wake up from this dream went unanswered. Neither could he force his brain to remember who he was, and pounding a fist against his temple didn't help. It seemed like hours until the door opened again.

The tall shadow of a standing crocodile fell on him. Another figure walked in as well, and the door closed once more.

"Markham?" That was Nina's voice.

Markham dragged himself to the surface of pillows, flumping them off his body. He heard Nina sigh.

"It's him," she said to the crocodile. By his bright green skin, Markham recognized it was Master Gavial. The less scary one.

Then something hit him in the face. He sputtered and grabbed it with one hand.

"Care to explain?" said Nina.

It was his shirt—the one she'd changed him out of. At first he couldn't tell what was wrong with it. Then he noticed a *K* embroidered into the sleeve.

Markham's mouth dropped. "What?"

"Being a Kloffer that magically appeared from the open ocean isn't a good look," said Nina. "You're lucky no one noticed it before."

Gavial clucked.

"Gavial agrees."

"A—Are you serious?" said Markham. "How the hell could I be a Kloffer?"

Gavial clucked again. But the crocodile did not look too concerned.

Now Nina stepped closer to Markham. He looked up at her from the floor.

"Gavial suggested we turn you in as a suspect in the case of the First Mate gone missing."

Markham just raised his eyebrows. He imagined the terror of being tried and jailed in a place like this. And with the Mariners gone, those three-inch-long teeth on Gavial might just be the judge and jury.

Nina crouched next to Markham. "I have a better idea."

Markham blinked.

"You help me find the First Mate and prove that he's all right," she said, "and we'll assume your innocence."

Gavial seemed pleased with that. His claws were crossed as usual behind his back.

"You think I'd be any help here?" said Markham.

Nina rolled her eyes. "Look, bycatch, you can walk out of here a murder suspect or you can come with me." She held out her hand. He stared at it.

"What's it gonna be?"

Nina plucked feathers off Markham as they walked away from the room. Gavial strolled in a leisurely pace in the opposite direction.

"Let me get this straight," said Markham.

Nina flicked off a feather. "Go on."

"Actually, question first," he said. "What even was that room?"

"A closet for screaming into pillows," said Nina matter-of-factly.

"I am beyond shocked I was alone in there," said Markham.

"Yes, it's usually crowded," said Nina. "Now what did you want to get straight?"

"Let me get this straight," Markham repeated. "You don't believe I'm really a gangster."

"Not at all," she said.

"Should that offend me?"

"A little," said Nina. "You're way too scrawny and clueless."

"Okay. But you're still going to force me to help you under threat of arrest?"

"I was doing you a favor. Would you rather skip right to the arrest?"

"No, but—"

"You may look innocent to me, but that doesn't matter. I just work for Gavial. This is his insistence."

Markham watched the crocodile lift a claw and wave at a group of passengers on his way down the stairs. While he wasn't an official authority, he certainly had popularity. And muscle.

"He seems to have thoughts on you I don't," said Nina, "and I trust him."

"And why do you want to find the First Mate so badly again?" said Markham.

"Find the First Mate, find the Captain," said Nina. She grasped her sand dollar amulet.

"And the Captain can end all this gangster stuff," Markham concluded. He glanced at her four-fingered hand again. Remembered the Kloffers warning her to pay them.

"Now you're sounding less clueless."

"You know, the whole doesn't-like-him-at-first cliché is really not vibing with me," said Markham.

"Who said this is just an at-first thing?" Nina spun to him. Her energy contradicted her words, however. There was a spark between them when she moved closer.

Markham shivered and gulped.

"I need to go check on something," she said. "Your job now is to get a room card in the Mess. I'll find you later."

"The Mess?" said Markham

"Big sign," said Nina. "Can't miss it."

And with that, she disappeared down the hall.

Sure enough, the Mess *was* pretty hard to miss—and only a few steps away.

Ahead of Markham rose an enormous arch like the entrance to an amusement park. Letters climbing along it spelled THE MESS.

Markham moved toward it with a river of passengers.

City opened up to him. He couldn't find the ceiling—the space just disappeared into what must have been artificial sky. Skyscrapers shot up and shimmered with golden lights. Tunnels connected the buildings and crossed over the blocks, their windows flashing as silhouettes moved through. Markham breathed in cool air and turned his head to the sad drone of a violin threading through the night. The violinist wore a trench coat with a high collar—their age, gender, and race impossible to determine—and leaned on the brick wall of a dark alley. The smell of stale alcohol and cat urine made Markham turn his head away and clutch his green robe closer.

Light from the building windows splashed onto the pavement, and Markham tilted his head back to read the protruding wire signs that buzzed with electricity. It took passing several of them—signs for breweries, dry cleaners, factories that oozed green slime—for Markham to realize what he was looking for: a building of some kind with a bed symbol. Even a hospital would do—anywhere for him to close his eyes again and make this place go away.

Soon he was swaying and the colors swirled into nothing. In his mind, the words *Markham Brody* flashed like a billboard on headlights. That was his name. Still, that and his age were all he remembered.

Then he froze. Somehow he'd walked far enough to find a brightly lit set of steps on his right, a revolving door atop them. The overhead sign read:

CHECK IN

Markham blinked. The sign buzzed. It flickered once.

He reached for the railing and climbed the steps.

Gold and brown blurred together as he spun through the revolving door. Like at any other hotel, first was the lobby. Tan tiled floor and paisley armchairs. Abandoned luggage sat upright against the wall. A pair of concierge shoes, polished but frayed, rested atop a shiny gold dolly. He surveyed the room as he walked in, but it seemed empty. Empty, except . . .

At the end of the lobby was the circular reception desk. A silver bell bid his welcome. No one attended it. An open archway stood just beyond, and past that . . .

Doors and doors. Rooms and rooms.

Markham dropped his newspaper and rushed for them like a runaway for water in the desert.

"You'll need a key, you know."

Markham nearly tripped turning towards the voice.

A rancher-type man sat on a chair at the wall, resting both hands on the handle of his suitcase. His grey moustache drooped on either side like a hairy dog's. He blinked slow and often. Snakes were engraved in the leather of his boots.

"I just . . ." Markham panted. "How do I get a room?"

"This is the check-in on the ship, son. And ain't nobody here to do it no more."

"There're vacant rooms though," said Markham, challenging rather than questioning.

The cowboy gave a long, deep nod. "Yessir, I reckon. Locked."

Markham shoved the back of his hand over his nose. "All right. Thanks." He began to make for the desk but stopped.

"What—What are you doing here?"

"I'ma be sittin' right here."

"Doing what?" said Markham.

"I'ma waitin', sir, yes I am."

"For what?" Markham pressed, annoyed.

"You'll see. E'er since this here ship sailed with *cotton sails,* I been a'waitin'."

"Cotton sails?"

"Yessir, an' oars before that."

"So, this ship gets renovated and stuff? Have we ever landed on shore?"

Hope tingled in Markham's chest. Maybe there was a port coming up he could escape to.

But the cowboy slapped his knee. "'Land?!'" He howled. "Boy, did you say *'land?!'*"

"Okay, thanks," said Markham.

"Funniest damn thing I e'er heard." He continued laughing. "Land."

Markham shook his head and approached the reception desk.

As soon as he chimed the bell and produced a sweet, resounding ting, a scroll popped from the desktop like a jack-in-the-box. He leaned forward to read it as the bell continued to vibrate on the counter. The words were sloppy and seemed handwritten in barbecue sauce. There were several misspellings and backwards letters.

Check in through door on left.

Markham did the obvious: looked at the door on the left.

He swallowed.

Bullets, or maybe termites (was that any better?), riddled the wooden door. There was no handle, only a doorknob hole. Scraped as if with a nail were the words Keep Out and several cusses. He pulled his brows together. This couldn't be right.

But what was the next best option? He'd fall over in exhaustion at any second and be left here with the deranged cowboy.

Check in. Just check in and sleep.

He moved for the vulgar entrance.

Just as his fingers looped into the hole in the door—

Oomph!

Jaws clamped over his leg and flipped him onto his back.

FOUR

It looked like Gavial. Its scaly throat lurched as it gnawed on Markham's leg. But its skin was brown.

Markham didn't scream. Survival instinct whammed his fist between the eye bumps of the crocodile's head. The monster thrashed left and right. His tail lashed into Markham's side. Using his elbows, Markham scrambled backwards and tried to jerk his leg from the beast's mouth. The crocodile snapped his jaws over it again, but before Markham's flesh could separate . . .

"GIT!"

An umbrella hit the brown crocodile over the head. The beast released Markham, flung around to the newcomer, and reared up on its hind legs. It pushed the person down. The person staggered but didn't fall, and the crocodile—Crocidius, Markham finally saw by the black clothing and the vertical-slit pupils of his eyes—

landed on his claws and shot off on his belly for the revolving door.

Markham coughed. Adrenaline kept the pain away for now, but his heart pounded.

"Well look at that vermin!" said his rescuer—the man with the umbrella. He was old and wrinkly with a cackling voice and dark skin. A striped black-and-white suit coat fell to nearly his knees, it was so oversized, and strange radio antennae stuck out from his collar and one shirt sleeve. "Gavial needs to get a muzzle on that ankle-biter. 'Scuse the pun." Yet the man doubled over hysterically. Tears sprang into his eyes. Markham stared at him in curved disbelief.

"Need a hand up?" The man finally straightened.

"Please," said Markham, not sure whether to be irritated or grateful.

The man raised his hand in the air like a student in class. Leaving Markham on the floor.

Again, the man burst into laughter. Markham grumbled as he helped himself to stand.

"Yeah, well, thanks for getting rid of him," said Markham.

"No problem, squirt. The name's Sylvester Andrews. Though most call me Syl. Or Silly. Get it?" Sylvester extended his hand. Markham stared at it for a critical beat, ensuring there were no pranks tied to his palm.

He took Sylvester's hand and pumped it.

Like his arm was a lever, Sylvester grew six inches with every pump. He jerked back his hand and squealed. "How embarrassing!"

Markham leapt back, his eyebrows shooting up.

"Oh, dear," said Sylvester, looking down at his pant sleeves, which were suddenly too short. "Pump this one, will you?" He held out his other arm.

Mouth open, Markham pumped the other hand, and Sylvester shrunk to normal height.

Sylvester sighed. "There. Sorry you had to see that. Now what's a squirt like you doing in this baaaaad neck of the woods?"

He bloomed open his umbrella with a giant *FLOOOOF!* Markham jumped back even farther.

"More importantly, why do you have an umbrella in an entirely indoor ship?" What Markham guessed to be entirely indoors. He hadn't explored it all yet.

Sylvester swung the umbrella over his shoulder. "Fashion." He twisted it around him like a supermodel.

"That's been extremely inconsistent from what I've seen so far."

"Bold fashion insults coming from someone in a bath robe!" Sylvester waved at Markham. "You ain't seen nothing yet."

"Why does everyone keep telling me that?" Markham breathed out, more to himself than anyone. He thought of Nina again.

"And I'd know a lot about seeing!" said Sylvester, as if he hadn't heard. "I'm a studio junkie responsible for *all* the Silly Channels—Blue Star Line's best and only broadcast pleasures! In fact . . ."

He pulled out a tiny radio from his striped jacket pocket and held it to his ear, twisting a knob that fanned out waves of static. At last, whale sounds moaned through eerie echoes.

"My newest show is on! *The Real Housewhales of—*"

"Right," said Markham. "I gotta get going . . ." He lifted a finger weakly at the graffitied door.

"Whoa, partner!" said Sylvester.

"*Yee-haw.*"

Sylvester turned towards the archway behind them, where the cowboy still sat in his chair, out of view. Markham peered past Sylvester's shoulder, and Sylvester and Markham exchanged a look.

"Wow. Let's try that again!" said Sylvester. He raised his voice. "WHOA, PART—"

"No," Markham interrupted. "Let's not try that again. I'm checking in, getting a room, and going to bed." He pushed past the man with the umbrella. But Markham lost his footing and fell backwards when Sylvester hooked his armpit with the umbrella handle and then caught him with one arm.

"I mean it," said Sylvester. "You don't wanna go in there, partner."

"*Yee-haw.*"

Still holding up Markham, Sylvester howled with laughter. "HE DID IT AGAIN!"

Angry now, Markham shoved him off with force.

"Hey—*ow!*" said Sylvester.

"I've been through *hell* today!" Markham straightened his shirt hard. "Just back off and let me through!"

"Well, don't get your handsome little whiskers in a tizzy!"

Markham ran a hand down his face subconsciously at that comment, feeling the growth of stubble. Did he always have stubble, or did the man he couldn't remember being shave?

"If you're so bent on going, well gosh dang it, loop her through!" Sylvester offered his arm as if to walk Markham down the aisle.

It was hopeless. Markham sighed. He wove his arm through and banged open the door.

Instantly the mood changed. There was a reason Sylvester had tried to stop him.

What they walked into resembled an eroded indoor ghetto. One streetlamp illuminated trash, paper, and rat droppings carpeting the pavement. About thirty yards ahead rose a cement wall with no visible top. But worse . . .

They were not alone.

Ahead was a simple desk with drawers. It looked as if it were dragged out of a cubicle and placed randomly in the middle of the street at the wall. Two people sat behind it—one a teenage boy with short black hair and dark skin like Sylvester, the other a teenage girl popping green bubble gum and snapping it around her teeth with an open mouth. Neither wore the sand dollar pendant Markham had come to think belonged to everybody. Their shirts had the *K* embroidered on their sleeves. But all in all, they didn't seem too threatening.

The debris on the ground was like a layer of fallen leaves. As Markham's feet shuffled through it, a charred black building to his right pulled his gaze.

Rusty gas pumps hung on hinges, and the walls of the fueling station were half-burnt. Under the roof of the station were two enormous figures—definitely not human, and standing on two hooves. Their skin was grey and oddly shaped, as if boulders fastened together to form a body. Scant, furry clothing covered them. Held in their hands, which were the size of skillet lids, were huge silver machine guns. The guns' enormous bottles were revolvers capable of spinning and firing several rounds at once. As if guarding something, the bull-men's brooding eyes turned to Markham and Sylvester. They watched Markham approach the desk. Thankfully it was too dark for them to make out Markham's bleeding leg, or anything of suspicion.

Seeing the fueling station allowed Markham to place his finger on the smell: a weird blend of sweet garbage and bitter gasoline. Trash crunched beneath Markham's shoes as he came up to the desk at last. Even Sylvester was wriggling his closed lips in discomfort. An unexpected surge of endearment and gratitude welled in Markham for this stranger who was escorting him for support.

"Can I help you?" said the boy. All attitude.

"I just need a room," said Markham. His voice echoed. His words were tight.

He glanced over to the left, where the street block turned a bend at another streetlamp. It was like looking down the path of a gnarled, dead forest. All Markham wanted to do was get away. Go back.

"Checking in for the first time, huh?" said the boy. The girl cracked her gum. "That's weird. What are you, eighty?"

"Twenty-six," said Markham, fast. He wanted to do this fast.

"Your hair looks like my grandfather's."

"Yeah, I know."

They stared at it. The girl popped her gum again.

"Look, can you just check me in?!" Markham snapped. He flinched the very next second, stealing a look over at the two huge gunmen without moving his neck. One was craning his trollish head around the charred stations, giving a *hrumph* like a bull.

"Geeez," said the boy. "Don't make me get Kloff out here." It seemed to have been a joke, but Markham narrowed his eyes as the boy arranged paperwork. *Kloff. Why would Kloff be doing the check-ins? Isn't that something the Captain's officials would . . . ?*

He remembered everything Nina had told him.

Bad parts of the ship . . .

The boy punched some quick stamps on paperwork and half

stood to hand Markham the documents and a plastic keycard. He pulled back at the last second.

"Oh yeah, what's your name again?"

"Markham Brody." That he never forgot.

The boy scribbled it down.

"And your reason for registering for a room?"

Markham paused. Reason for registering? Don't they all have rooms? But then he thought of the homeless in the elevator, the violinist in the alley. The hotel.

"I can afford it now," he blurted.

Even Sylvester shot him a look for that one. Markham swallowed. He hoped Nina had a plan to cover this since she instructed him to come here. If not, he'd just have to get off this ship before the debt found him.

The boy gave a sharp "*Ha!*" He extended the papers towards Markham again. "There you go!" said the boy brightly.

"Bye," said the girl. Gum stretched over her face, but she didn't bother raising a hand to remove it. Markham had never been so sure that the Kloff shirt he arrived in had absolutely nothing to do with him.

"Mmmmmmm let's get out of here now, squirt . . ." Sylvester began to tug at him. Markham walked backwards at his insistence but didn't object. He looked down at his document—Welcome Aboard!—in disbelief.

Just as they reached the exit, the two bull-guards began to rumble, watching after them.

"*Phew!*" said Sylvester, closing the door behind them. "I'm glad that's over with. That right there's why homelessness's gone up since Kloff overtook the check-in process."

"Shouldn't the Captain oversee things like that?" said Markham.

He stuffed his keycard into his pocket and stooped to retrieve the newspaper he had dropped what seemed like hours ago.

"Well, he yousta," said Sylvester. He pulled a long, rainbow-colored tourniquet from his sleeve like a clown would. Markham accepted it and began wrapping his bitten leg, which had just begun to hurt now that he wasn't shaking with nerves. He gritted his teeth. Sylvester continued. "Then First Mate Yastley started taking more an' more a . . . er, *back seat,* and they shut down all the check-in offices an' the Mariners sorta rotted off and—"

"And now we're all—"

"No interruptin'! And the gangs crept in to take over the business and collect the tax and no one's seemed to stop them yet." Sylvester took a deep breath after the run-on sentence.

"Is there more than one Kloff? More mob lords?" said Markham.

"Oh, sure's! This is just one little turf. You got Kloff, Obensteen, Babsy . . . just stay away from them all, little croc-bait!" He paused, then pointed at the keycard. "Except, I guess you'll be paying Kloff now. Seems to be he's got a monopoly on the room biz, an' you just bought in. It charges to that there keycard."

"How much is it a day?"

Sylvester frowned, which looked especially unsettling on him.

"Under the Captain it was only twenty clams a day." He scratched his head. "Somethin' like a hundred now."

Markham blinked. He didn't even want to think about what he'd have to do on this ship to earn *clams.* Nope. He had to get off.

"Anyhoo!" Sylvester slapped him on the back—that was two slaps in one day for Markham—and moseyed off towards the revolving door, swinging his opened umbrella at his side.

"Silly!" Markham called.

Sylvester turned, truly surprised, eyebrows raised.

"Thank you," Markham said.

Sylvester smiled. He purposefully tripped into the revolving door, and it twirled him away.

Ding!

Markham glided into the elevator, reading the dorm number on his keycard. Without looking up, he punched a button with his thumb and leaned onto the wall. Sighing.

The elevator sucked upwards.

His leg ached, but the bleeding had stopped, and the wound wasn't as deep as he'd first thought. In just a few moments, the elevator slowed, and Markham lifted his eyes from the keycard. He did a double take at the buttons.

Deck 58 was alight. He'd meant to press 52, the button directly below.

Uh oh.

The elevator leveled with the floor, and Markham glanced at the handful of other humanoid passengers in the lift with him. They were backing into the corners of the elevator. Markham's muscles coiled.

With an eerily normal *ding*, the elevator doors rolled open.

A metal barricade—just a firm black wall with a few planks of wood—faced them, so no one could exit. In white spray paint KLOFF! was written at the top, and below it, SALUTE THE "K"APTAIN!

Unnerving silence rang. But occasionally, somewhere beyond the barricade in the distance . . . tiny sounds echoed. Debris crumbling. Something ticking slowly. The empty keen of seething air.

The passengers with Markham exchanged worried looks. They could only wait for the doors to close again.

The doors did, with the spooky sound of a train moving slowly over tracks. Markham pressed the correct button this time and swallowed.

"Sorry," he said softly. No one replied.

He rubbed his exhausted eyes as the elevator began to move again.

Later, Markham knocked his keycard against the scanner, missing twice as if drunk. He was on the 52nd floor now, ten stories above the Mess. When the card finally swept through and the room lock beeped, Markham stumbled in. He smacked facedown onto the mattress, not lucid enough to even take in the cabin's surroundings, and like one unbroken dial tone slept through the night.

Until a loud, pounding knock rattled the door.

FIVE

Blankets fell off Markham as he rose from the bed. He dragged his hand down his face and labored for the door.

"I changed my mind."

The words came as soon as he'd opened it. Nina barged into his cabin as if it were her own. Markham staggered back.

"I decided I might like you at first," said Nina. She dropped a bundle of clothes and brown boat shoes onto his bed and moved for the porthole window in the back of the cabin.

"You have a city view," she stated, as if this should be encouraging. Markham picked up the clothes and looked in her direction.

"What?"

"Your window. It looks out over the Mess."

"Uh, yeah. What other views are there?" Markham yawned.

"Well . . ." She ran her fingers around the circle window.

"Okay, so, it's a sixty-deck ship. That I know of. Decks one to twenty are all underwater views. The draft is deep cuz—"

"The tonnage is so huge?" said Markham.

"Yeah," said Nina.

"What are all the other decks?" Markham placed his hands on his hips.

"I wasn't finished," snapped Nina. "The galley is the bottom floor, but there're whole technical decks below which only the Captain can access. Pretty much all of the others have residences. But off the top of my head . . . Deck 25 is the casino and the hospital."

"Practical combo," said Markham.

"Deck 29 has the sauna. It's more like a large spa, but it's steamed and has a pool. Greenhouses are on the entire outer ring of the thirtieth deck. Deck 34 has the movie theater and the studios. Forty-two is the Mess, which goes up several more decks . . . Deck 60 is the Captain's Parlor. It's sort of like a fancy ballroom in his honor. And that's it, mostly."

"Mostly?"

"Well. You know." She sat on his bed in a huff. "There are decks above that which only the Captain and First Mate can reach. Fifty-nine is wealthy estates, and there's also a little stage off it, right below the parlor balcony, for the First Mate to make his appearances . . ."

Markham hesitated. "What about Deck 58?" He remembered the looks the passengers in the elevator had shared on that floor.

Nina's tone darkened. "That used to be the administrative deck. It had the courthouse, the treasury . . ."

"Health Bureau?" Markham suggested. It really looked like they needed one.

Nina nodded. "Office of the First Mate . . . all in gold . . ."

Markham turned his head curiously and watched her.

"Kloff shut down that entire deck last week. Every Mariner at the Mariner Department was killed or ran off."

Markham blinked. "Wow."

"They—the gangsters—camp out there now—who knows how many. I told you, it's not good," said Nina. "But yeah. There are a million other things. You'll never explore every corner of this ship. You'll die first."

Markham shook his head. "How did you find me then?"

"I checked the directory at the phone booth. Though I was a little surprised you registered so fast."

"I mean . . ." Markham said.

"Rent is due the first of the month," said Nina. "Gavial agreed to cover you so long as you keep to our deal. And rent is collected by Kloff's men now, so, you know . . . I'd keep the deal."

There was a pause. He glanced at her four-fingered hand.

Nina continued gazing out his window.

"What is your view?" Markham spoke in a more relaxed tone, realizing she wouldn't be leaving anytime soon. But why would he ever want her to? She felt like an anchor in this bizarre new world, her chain going taut and keeping him from lurching. Still listening for her reply, Markham sidestepped into the closet and finally replaced his robe with the normal, comfortable clothes she'd brought: khaki pants and a black Hawaiian shirt. A floral pattern contrasted the black, and coconut-shell buttons studded down the center.

"The casino. Room 215." Nina sighed. "I wish it were . . ."

He stepped out. Nina turned.

A long pause.

"What?" said Markham.

"The ocean. Underwater."

Markham studied her. He waited for her to go on.

"When I see into the deep blue, I just . . . feel something . . ." She still wasn't looking at him. "Like I know something out there that I don't know in here."

He thought about that.

But then she coursed for him so fast that he reversed in reflexiveness.

Her hands dove into his silver hair, and he backed into the drawers and steadied himself against them, prepared for whatever physical extremity she was about to do to him. She didn't kiss him though, just felt him, moved her hands down to scrape his shadow and then down his shoulders to his chest.

He shook.

"You hardly know me." His voice was breathy.

"I know you better than anyone on this ship," said Nina.

His Caribbean-blue eyes strained down to follow the trail of her fingers. She dropped her voice to a whisper.

"We're not like them."

He swallowed.

But was he like her?

Just as abruptly, Nina snapped her eyes up to him as if she'd said nothing before.

"I want to show you something."

She punched the button to the sixtieth floor. Short a ride as it'd be, Markham still sat beneath the rack of elevator buttons and massaged his head. He chewed on the two mild painkillers Nina had offered him like breath mints.

"I'm sorry about your leg," said Nina. Markham had wrapped it in a new towel from the bathroom before they left. "I called Dr. Flabberstein, but he can't see you until this afternoon."

"Where are we heading?" said Markham. "Is this the lead you were checking up on?"

All around were squeaks on the glass of the elevator; snail janitors clung to the walls and scrubbed the glass with sponges attached to their eye stems.

"About the First Mate missing," he added.

Nina's voice got small. "Not . . . exactly."

"What were you checking on, then? What was the lead?"

"I . . . don't have a lead, Markham," said Nina.

Markham stopped.

"I left to get you the new clothes. That's all."

All at once the sweetness of that and the horror of it hit Markham. Nina, in fact, had no idea where to start.

"What does the First Mate normally do?" said Markham. It seemed like a good time to take initiative.

"He actually speaks to us. It's televised on every Silly Channel on the ship. Or in person, if you want to stand there with the reporters. Deck 59. Remember?"

"So he knows who the Captain is?"

"Not necessarily." Nina reached down and pulled Markham to stand as the elevator slowed. "But he definitely communicates with him. Whether it's over coffee or through a wall, I don't know."

Markham brushed himself off, looking around as the suds wept down the glass from the sponges, then followed Nina. "So if all the First Mate does is relay and enforce the Captain's command, what makes you so sure he's not the Captain in disguise? Maybe he doesn't want the attention."

This deck of the ship, compared to those below, was oddly formal. Tall curtains fell on either side of the fifteen-foot, floor-to-ceiling windows that looked out over the endless ocean. Dawn's light raked over pink and yellow clouds that looked like they'd been mowed over with a lawn mower. The green ocean feasted on the light. Only a few stately people roamed the floor, hands crossed behind or in front of them as they rotated from window to window as if contemplating their next poetic composition. Their shoes echoed and squeaked over shiny rose-colored marble, and the silence of the place, the hushed reverence, put Markham on edge.

"Because he's not the only First Mate in history," Nina answered. "The last one had a heart attack three years ago. The ones before that have been fired. Tell me about a Captain that would fire himself."

"One who realized the pressure was too much."

"What pressure? No one knows who you are."

"Maybe the Captain actually cares about the people he looks after." Strangely, Markham's words seemed to bite. Nina glanced at him sideways. "What are you showing me?" he added in annoyance, as if to deter the subject.

"That."

In the center of the floor, right before the center balcony that opened up to the dozens of stories below, was a life-sized glass display case.

One old woman with a pink shawl around her head knelt at the case. She looked up, lifted a spotted, knobby hand, and saluted the case for a long time. It wasn't until she slowly hauled herself to stand and hobbled away that Markham approached close enough to see what was inside.

A handsome, dignified Captain's hat—gold ivy along the visor, iridescent naval anchor stitched into the white fabric—rested atop a masculine dark jacket. Gold anchor-and-rope buttons studded down the jacket's center in double columns. Four gold stripes barred the sleeve cuffs on either side. Shoulder boards jutted out and looked both fatherly and fierce. On the chest of the mannequin hung a live, fuzzy green sand dollar framed in gold and etched with the anchor crest of the Captain.

"Wow." Markham's voice was an unintentional whisper.

"That's his."

Markham couldn't help but look over at Nina in sharp curiosity. The tone of her voice clearly resonated hopeful love. "The Captain's," stated Markham.

She nodded.

"He wears that sand dollar thing, too," Markham continued. "What's that about?"

"They're delivered to all of us mysteriously after we're born," said Nina. "Everyone's is a little different—they're like our real names. They're his gift to us, but also mark our loyalty, and they can't be lost or broken by someone else unless we choose to give it up or break it ourselves."

Markham remembered the snapped-in-half sand dollar hanging from Crocidius' neck. He'd chosen to sever his for some reason.

"Can you trade them?" said Markham.

"If you try to wear one that's not yours," said Nina, "It will burn your skin and brand you forever. The only way to get rid of them is intentionally.

"If enough of us give them up," she continued, "legend says the elements won't obey him anymore. They start out fresh and green from the sea. And whiten and dry as we age."

Markham pointed to the case. "Isn't that one supposed to be really old, if the Captain's been the Captain forever? His sand dollar is still green."

"Symbolizing his immunity to age," said Nina, as if this should be obvious. She touched her own fading-green talisman again.

And then Nina moved to the glass and pressed her hand against it. Markham kept his distance, reading the words on the dark grey plaque beneath the mannequin.

I give my uniform to you, passengers, as a reminder of my everlasting presence and love. I need it not where I am. You need it wherever you are.

Markham couldn't decide whether the sentences were affectionate or imposing.

"Sometimes I stare into the case and look at my reflection against it, imagining I'm wearing the clothes," said Nina.

"Would you want to steer this ship?" Markham came up next to her, keeping his head down in bashful respect of what seemed to be important to her.

But she laughed. Harshly. Almost judgmentally.

"No."

She spun back to him in her sudden way. And left just as quickly.

Markham caught his reflection in the case before following after her. He saw the hat above his head, the gold buttons glimmering down his front. The shoulders were powerful; the sleeves were long. A moment passed. He turned away.

Nina was already waiting for the elevator to go back down.

"We're already leaving. You showed that to me why?" he said.

"I don't know," she replied. Crossed her arms.

"Okay," said Markham. Long silence stretched between them. "Nina?" he said.

She pressed him with her abrupt gaze. It almost disarmed him of his sentence.

"In the newspaper article, it said the Captain's last message came three months ago."

"Yeah?" She shrugged standoffishly.

"What did it say?"

Nina pursed her lips, then shifted them side to side. The elevator doors aligned with the floor and slowed.

"He just reminded us to follow him and trust him."

Markham narrowed his eyes. "Were those his exact words?"

The doors sprang open. Nina spoke without looking back.

"He said '*Seek me.*'"

SIX

"Ahhh . . . ahhh . . ." Markham seethed every time he stepped using the foot Crocidius had gnawed.

Nina squeezed his arm, which was wrapped in hers. "Yeah, well, idiots who don't treat flesh wounds pay later on."

"Can you have a talk with Gavial?" said Markham. They traveled through a bright metal hall. He looked at the labels on each curved, submarine-like door as they passed. Their footsteps clinked like hail on a windowpane.

"No," said Nina. Remorseless.

"Thanks," said Markham in a sigh.

Nina turned to him. "I said no."

Markham looked over almost dolefully.

"Crocidius is like that, Markham." Nina shrugged. "I don't exactly know why he bit you, but they're still . . ."

"Crocodiles?"

"Master Gavial is only a quarter gavial. He's very sensitive about that," she chided.

"Um. Okay. Are there any other adult crocodiles on the ship?" said Markham.

"Just them."

"He has kids, though," said Markham. "What happened to Mrs. Gavial?"

"There was a shortage of handbags one year," said Nina. "We don't talk about it. Here we are."

She steered him to a watertight door on their left and turned the wheel but didn't push it open. A symbol of steam rising from a tub was painted onto the door.

"I'll leave you here," said Nina. "I have to work dinner tonight."

Markham nodded without looking up from his glossy, dressed leg wound. "Are you sure I need to go into the sauna? Is saltwater really a good idea on this?"

"Dr. Flabberstein is never wrong," said Nina.

"Dr. Flabberstein was a vending machine."

"And did the ointment he popped out work?" Nina challenged.

Markham pulled up his pant sleeve and twisted his leg around. Skin had already begun to heal, and pain struck only when he laid weight on it. He sighed.

Then he remembered something.

"Wait, if Dr. Flabberstein is a vending machine, *why wasn't he able to see me until this afternoon.*"

"I'll meet you tonight," said Nina, as if she hadn't heard. "Don't forget. Tunnel of Chemically Induced Hormones."

"Really?" said Markham, exasperated. "'Love' doesn't work for anybody?"

"We'll see." Nina's voice was suddenly low, and her glance showed a flash of sheepishness.

They kissed. Markham pressed forward as far as he could, until his shoe tips hit the wall behind her. Lust spiked through him. By some unknown instinct, he suppressed it. This kiss was tender, more exploratory and emotive than the others. For a moment, he thought he felt something different in her lips, in the soft movement of her throat.

Then she ripped away.

"NUH UH! NO!" Nina looked over his shoulder at something. He spun.

Lined up against the metal wall in a single row were the tiny black frogs again. Their eyes were as wide and absorbed as the first time.

Nina stormed around Markham and shooed them away with kicks. They slopped off, leaving inky marks in their wake.

"WHERE do they come from?!" Nina huffed and coursed down the hall without a single glance back. She thundered up a grated staircase and out of view. Markham was alone again.

He geared his courage and turned for the curved sauna door, then pushed it in.

Steam rose in clouds and clung to the hairs on his arms like dew on grass. He reeled in furls of moisture. The heavy door sealed him in from behind.

Ahead was a hot pool. Lights wriggled beneath the water like churning rods of lightning. Opaque white orbs lit the tile around the spring, but all was dim. Figures slugged like zombies around the water's edge. Both the left and right walls were pure glass, revealing a dark, murky aquarium. Fish the size of whales lurked between seaweed and slid into shadow. Markham gulped.

Were they decoration or passengers?

Markham moved to a changing stall next to a bearded bust of a godlike figure with a jutting chin and waves along his crown. Complimentary sturdy nylon swim trunks sat folded on a shelf, all grey, all identical. He hung his black cabana shirt on a hanger. Unbuckled his belt. Kept his eyes away from anyone but himself.

Soak the wound. Get out, he thought. He approached the steaming green water. Someone—something—burst from the deep spring in front of him. It mounted the steps as water streamed loudly off it and back into the pool. The lumpy, hunched thing moved as slowly as everything else in here, but Markham thought he caught the flare of gills beneath the collar it wore. His breath hitched, memories of being in the frothing seafood tank in the galley dumping back into him.

Using both hands on the rim behind him for support, Markham inched into the hot water.

Salt stung his leg. He took in a sharp breath. But then it ebbed, and pleasure shuddered up his body. The heat soothed him. He sunk in lower.

The water heater at the wall facing him flashed digital numbers as a giant brown fish swam past seaweed on the other side of the glass behind it. The gigantic fish disappeared into the aquatic forest.

Markham jerked at every lapping of dark water against him. Expecting a shark. A tentacle. Anything. But nothing ever came. The sauna echoed with casual human laughter by the changing stalls, and Markham relaxed. A pair of middle-aged businessmen walked around the edge of the pool and slid their hands on the rails to walk in. They didn't pay the slumping, amphibian-like zombies a second glance. One amphibian even bowed its head as it passed them.

Machine, man, and beast. Every twisted passenger on this ship seemed to have a touch of soul. Markham's shoulders relaxed.

Then, something tickled his side. Markham thrashed away, rocking the water around him, and looked down. Gold particles glittered in a thread of stringy silver seaweed. He grasped the thread, feeling its silkiness slip through his palm.

Far at the other end of the pool, almost a hundred yards away, something growled.

Every bather froze. They looked over at the noise.

A lone bather, heaped in brown clothes and hidden behind jazzy sunglasses of endless blue, emitted a rumble so ominous and low that bubbles pattered all around the edges of the pool. A large tsunami pendant glimmered in the water around his neck. His grey beard seeped into the water and stretched out like roots of a great oak, longer, longer . . .

Markham swallowed and looked down at his fist. He released the grey seaweed—*the beard tendril.*

The rumbling stopped.

After a tense moment, everyone chuckled. Except Markham. He sloshed a soggy hand onto his forehead in relief and shakiness as if to say, *Holy crap.*

That was his cue to go. He waltzed through the water towards the stairs. When his foot reached the first dry step, he looked up at the door. A steam cloud rolled away to reveal a bipedal reptilian figure stalking in, a towel draped over its arm. Markham's heart pounced into his throat. It was too dim to see the shade of its scales . . . green or brown?

After a few more steps, the brightness of the crocodile's shiny black eyes shone and reflected the water. The easy buoyancy of his gait became more visible. Markham should have known by that alone; Crocidius preferred the traditional four-legged travel.

Master Gavial melted onto his stomach and into the pool. He adopted the lither, more foreboding movement of his cousin, snaking from side to side into the warm water. He relaxed his arms and legs, letting them drift back as he cruised forth. His eyes seemed to glaze over in pleasure with his tail becoming a rudder.

Markham released a tumbling sigh.

And then it hitched once more when the sparse lights cut to blackness.

The natural sounds of the water seemed louder in the pure darkness. Markham looked around for a source, any source, and when the opaque orbs flickered just once in the pool, he caught sight of Gavial. Stiff as a plank, Gavial's black-yet-bright eyes were pointed to the ceiling, where banging and scuffling sounds echoed through a vent. He no longer seemed relaxed but tense, with humanistic worry in his posture. The other bathers murmured, slogs of them swinging out of the water in curiosity, slapping around the perimeter.

And then, behind the sunglass-wearing, bearded bather at the end of the pool, a *crash* of drywall showered to the floor. If Gavial had eyebrows, they'd have lowered. He plunged like a torpedo beneath the water and emerged seconds later at the other end. Markham tore up the rest of the stairs and raced after him.

A squawk of horror trumpeted from Gavial like Markham had never heard before. The ceiling was completely broken through—the water-resistant wood covering the drywall splintered apart, even the metal from the vent torn open. But Gavial gaped down at something else, and Markham froze, shivering as water coursed from his body to the tile.

Sitting on top of a bed of drywall and a pool of blood was a brown crocodile claw.

SEVEN

"Yeah . . . he acted troubled in the kitchen, but he was functional. He mustn't think he's dead. What did he do after he saw the claw?"

Markham shuffled down pale yellow stairs on some hallway of the ship with Nina. He hesitated.

"I mean, I thought he was gonna eat it."

The smile creasing Nina's lips was almost endeared.

"He gathered it in his jaw and sped from the sauna. He looked . . . sad. Like he was frowning."

"Crocodiles can't frown," said Nina.

"I don't know about that after tonight."

They turned a bend. Two levels of conference rooms, their white doors stacked like book spines in a library, greeted them. At first Markham wondered how anyone accessed the top doors, but then one opened and a flood of horseshoe crabs with feathered wings flew out. They were wearing tiny little top hats and clutching briefcases. Markham ducked to avoid one that had an injured wing.

The injured horseshoe crab bobbed through the air lower and lower until it fell and tumbled across the ground, landing on its back. Its briefcase fell and miniature papers with pictographs Markham couldn't understand spilled out.

"Oh no!" said Nina. "Poor little guy." She rushed up to the crab as its spidery legs curled inward, almost as if embarrassed. Markham attempted to pinch the tiny papers in his fingers and stuff them back into the doll-sized briefcase.

"Should we get that thing to Dr. Flabberstein?" he said.

"*That thing* is a flying horseshoe crab and it has a name."

"I'm sorry," said Markham, nodding. "What's his name?"

"Well I don't know it but he has one," said Nina.

Markham smiled. He gently pinched shut the briefcase as Nina turned the crab onto its belly again.

Immediately the creature attempted to fly once more, but once more it dipped down on its injured side.

Markham knelt next to it. "Can I see?" he said.

The creature, on the floor again, just paced in a small circle, its shell wobbling. Markham touched the wing with his hand and saw the fracture of bone.

"It looks like he had some important business to get to with his friends," said Nina.

"He's not flying anywhere on this." Markham frowned.

"We can walk him in their direction, then," said Nina. "We were going that way anyway." She lifted the horseshoe crab onto her shoulder, and it clung there dutifully. Markham popped its top hat back on and handed the horseshoe crab its briefcase. They resumed their way forward.

The carpet below Markham's feet was deep red, like in a theater. Ahead, stairs ascended. But soon Markham and Nina began to weave through a crowd, shifting their shoulders. The flow of passengers was overwhelming for such a boring part of the ship, and traffic moved in two strict lines in opposite directions: one up the stairs, the other down.

"This is weird," said Markham. "I thought we were going to the Tunnel of Chemically Induced Hormones tonight."

"I forgot the Tunnel is sold out for another week. It's amphibian mating season."

"Wow."

They began to climb the stairs with the mindless current of passengers, Markham trusting Nina's lead. Someone lifted their hand and high-fived the old guy trundling down the stairs in the opposite direction, yet neither acknowledged the other or even looked over, their expressions dull.

"Well, something's got to keep the generations on this ship going for the Captain."

"Amphibian mating season though. That'll get you in the mood."

"What mood?" Nina looked over at him sharply. The horseshoe crab just bobbled on her shoulder.

Markham stuttered.

"Are you in the mood?" Her words were direct and fast, glancing him over as if she would do something about it if he were.

"I—" Markham blinked. They started going down a different flight of stairs.

"It's okay," said Nina, snapping out of it and looking forward again. They were still in the train of passengers. "You're not ready anyway."

Markham pulled an indignant face. "I'm like ten years older than you."

"Age doesn't matter. You're too sweet. You can't talk dirty."

Markham barked out a laugh that made the others around him glance over.

"I can—"

"Don't embarrass yourself."

"You go then," said Markham. "Right now."

She shot out a hand and grabbed his collar. He stumbled against her, still keeping pace with the group. Her hand continued to clench his shirt collar, and the other, four-fingered, one came up to grasp the front.

"I want everything inside of you that you can't stomach."

A shiver. Humor evaporated from him unexpectedly.

All right. He liked that.

Markham leaned down to kiss her. She shoved him away hard with one hand and he staggered again. Nina scoffed. "Amateur."

They reached the end of this staircase.

"Bye, little guy," said Nina, letting the horseshoe crab off her shoulder. They watched as it moseyed—walking—towards a little hole in the wall just big enough for a skateboard to get through. Other flying horseshoe crabs were landing and taking off there. Nina pulled Markham along and they turned at another left bend.

"Wait, what is this?" said Markham a few steps later. The same exact room opened before them, the one where they first found the injured horseshoe crab. "Do these people just walk around in circles all day?"

They mounted the far stairs once again.

"It's exercise," said Nina. "And yeah. Some do."

The same old men high-fived at the same spot, again looking forward blankly.

Then a deep, loud ocean-liner horn sounded through the building. Markham looked around for the source.

"Oh, good," said Nina. She tugged him by the elbow as a few others also broke free of the carousel. They headed for another—grey, now—flight of stairs, one that wouldn't lead in circles.

Nina pounded the up button on the giant glass elevator before Markham even scaled the grey stairs into the hall that rung around the elevator. Stationed against the walls here were clothed tables; gamblers sat on stools and leaned over mini roulette wheels. Markham and Nina must have ended up on Deck 25, the casino, and these little tables must have been just the sleepy overflow of gamblers who couldn't take the jingle and lights of the real place somewhere on this deck.

Nina ignored them and jittered on her heels, waiting for the lift. Markham came up to her, and the crowd waiting for the elevator tripled with passengers, so much so that the accumulated body heat was hot.

"Was that horn a big deal?" he said.

"Huge deal," said Nina.

The elevator opened and everyone piled in.

Wood gleamed on the floor, on the high stage, and at the podium. Below the podium was the thick gold seal of an anchor and rope, identical to those on the buttons of the Captain's jacket.

Hopeful and excited chatter filled the room. The pockets of

conversation were not limited to one species each, with alien listeners that seemed to understand English, grunts and gurgles which humans responded to with nods.

Past this lacquered gathering stage was the open drop of the elevator. Silhouettes hung at the rails of the halls from many levels. The farthest across the way were just dots.

Markham stood next to Nina and looked around.

"Everyone's acting like nothing's wrong." His statement was meant to be reassuring but seemed the opposite upon delivery.

"They're hoping nothing really is," said Nina.

"He does this every month? At this exact date and time?"

"Religiously."

"And the horn sounds automatically, or it's manually rung by the Captain?"

"We think automatic."

"But the First Mate hasn't come out the past two times?"

"No." Nina would not make eye contact with him.

Markham let the silence fall between them. Across bunches of passengers, someone waved to him manically. Dark skin, umbrella in hand. Markham broke out a smile and waved back to his savior, Sylvester.

Sylvester then turned to his short, golem-like companion and reenacted Markham's flip after Crocidius' strike and burst into laughter. The golem burbled with chuckles that caused pebbles to trickle from his chin. Markham rolled his eyes.

Around Sylvester were several sets of cameras and microphones, all stenciled with SILLY CHANNEL 1, SILLY CHANNEL 2, up until twelve. Or at least that's all Markham saw. Crew workers wearing headphones tilted their craned microphones closer.

When Markham's gaze traveled back to Nina, her expression

was still resting in serious lines, eyes touched with poorly disguised worry. He figured he'd better change the subject from the First Mate.

"So, do *you* think Crocidius is okay? You haven't seen him since."

"I know he's alive," said Nina. "And I know who attacked him. I just don't know why."

Markham repulsed in shock. "You know who attacked him."

"Of course," said Nina, still not looking at him. "Kloff's men." After a pause, she explained. "I know how they punish."

She tightened her four fingers into a fist at her breast.

Markham clenched his jaw. His voice was soft and low. "Why did they do that to you?"

Now she turned her head entirely away from him under the pretense of still looking around. "You have to survive on this ship, Twenty-Six."

Goosebumps rose along his neck.

The podium remained bare. No sign of First Mate Yastley.

As twenty, thirty minutes passed, the crowd's murmurs became concerned. Those with watches checked them.

And by an hour's passing, sadness and fear quieted all, and the polished wood floor showed more and more space as passengers left.

At the second hour's passing, Nina and Markham were the last ones standing in the middle of the floor.

Just as Markham raised a hand to lay it comfortingly on Nina's shoulder, ask her to leave with him, she jerked towards him. Her words snapped.

"Take me to where the claw fell."

EIGHT

Markham turned to her. Nina raised her eyebrows. An awkward pause followed.

"You can't go any farther, right?" said Markham. The curved door to the men's sauna was beside them: the same room with the pool, where everything had happened the night before.

Nina's arms were crossed and she looked at the door. "What are we, in second grade?"

"Not anymore, that's the point . . ."

She ignored him and twisted the door open. Markham patted his wrist against his side and followed her in, hoping no one would notice her. On this ship, gender seemed a little subjective, anyway. But with her . . .

He breathed in the hot moisture. In regular clothes, the sauna seemed soupier than normal. Dampness collected in the seams of tile beneath their feet. Mist veiled the dim, opaque orb lights around the room as always, but it was eerier than before. Being close to midnight, no one was bathing. The fallen drywall at the end of the long spring hadn't been cleaned. Nina spotted it and led the way with confident strides.

Markham's eyes jerked onto a familiar figure. They weren't alone after all . . .

That unnaturally long-bearded passenger was in his exact same spot in the pool at the end. Motionless. Seeming to stare ahead with his blue sunglasses and letting his grey beard spiral and writhe in the water. Beams of yellow spotlights cut through the brown murk to illuminate the beard tendrils.

"He was here before."

"Maybe he's aquatic," Nina replied, not even looking over at him.

Then Markham saw a pair of occupants he also hadn't noticed. They stood in a dark corner next to a table of oxygen masks—for diving, perhaps—and looked over at their approach. They were four-feet high and pirate-like: their prick ears chipped and skin mulberry colored. Black leather and chains dangled from them, and they were wet as if they'd just utilized the masks. Upon seeing Nina, they looked at one another and laughed in low, devious manners. Their eyes were bright orange.

Crocidius' blood stained the drywall pile like vanilla in flour. Nina hugged herself in uncharacteristic vulnerability and studied it. She raised her eyes to the broken ceiling several times.

Markham had nothing more to see here. Instead, he continued to pat his side with his wrist and cut his gaze around protectively.

Those two in the corner looked more and more interested in Nina.

"Come on," Markham prodded.

"Why would it happen here? What is right above us?" Nina wondered aloud.

"A vent?" Markham snapped, on edge. "Doesn't he travel that way?" The memory of Crocidius scrambling up the wall and into a vent on all fours in Gavial's kitchen came back to him. It was a striking thing to witness for his first day on board. Then again, almost everything was.

She looked at him. "What's your problem?"

"I think midnight is not the time to be out around here," he said.

Nina took a quick glance around to see if she agreed. Her melted arrogance and quiet seemed to confirm that she did.

Markham took her elbow.

The door to the sauna burst open. They all—including the two pirates—looked over.

Nina tucked her four-fingered hand against herself. It was the same two Kloff gangsters who had terrorized them at dinner. Huge, round, and with too much bare at their stomachs, they trundled in with wide, side-to-side gaits. They wore those hideous bandanas around their flat, volcanic heads this time.

"WHO IS HE?!" one boomed, voice rebounding around the sauna like a cannonball. The mulberry-skinned pirates emerged from the darkness of the corner table and bared their teeth, approaching like alley cats.

"You seek the mob lord who stole almighty Kloff's magic keys?" one pirate hissed.

"That's what Kloff gets for spending his time chewing the hand off some gecko," said the other pirate.

"OBENSTEEN'S COWARD . . . COWARD HE'S!"

Foxlike smiles twisted the mulberry pirates' faces. Markham noticed the tattooed *O*'s on their arms. He backed farther against the wall, holding out a hand to press Nina back with him.

"MOB LORD WHO STAY HIDDEN!" Kloff's gangster cried. "WHAT MOB LORD THAT?" Nina's eyes were closed in fear, but behind the defense of Markham, no one saw her.

"Smart one," replied Obensteen's crony.

"WHOEVER IS OBENSTEEN, WE FIND OUT!"

"Good luck."

The two sides growled and slobbered at one another for a few beats, and then Kloff's men turned and wobbled out of the sauna, sidestepping to fit through the door.

Markham released a sigh. He squeezed Nina's hand, and she squeezed back instantly.

"Let's go."

Ziiiip!

Markham swished closed the blinds. It was the first thing he did upon entering his cabin. He needed to shut out the ship for a good five- or six-hours' sleep. No dreams. Blackness.

When dawn crept up too fast, he awoke with a gasp. But nothing was there. Maybe he dreamed after all.

Next to him, on the nightstand, was a copy of *The Captain's Log,* a sacred text complimentary to every room, he guessed. A pair of glasses sat atop it, which he'd slipped on the night before to read a few pages. The prose read like flowery double-talk.

Markham sighed, not yet wanting to rise. He flopped out a hand and grabbed the remote control for the tube TV on the wall and pressed power.

He flipped through different Silly Channels, all featuring

Sylvester himself in some form, whether as news anchor, Latin soap opera uncle, or telesalesman. Markham stopped at a station with Sylvester sitting on a white couch, and two one-inch-long sardines lying on the cushion next to him as if dead.

"Sergio," said Sylvester. "You ARE NOT the father!"

The camera cut to the audience—a crowd of little silver sardines on rising seating levels—as it erupted with jumping and writhing fish bodies. One flew up and slapped itself onto the camera lens, covering it with a wide blank eyeball, while Sylvester shouted for order.

Markham groaned and turned off the screen.

He rose and rubbed his eyes, heading for the wardrobe to trade his black Hawaiian shirt for a ruby silk one, surfboards and tourist vans patterned all over it. He held it up on its hanger, contemplated it cynically, then shrugged and put it on.

Markham stepped out of his dorm and into the hall. The morning batch of creatures strolling by seemed tamer and more leisurely. Long yawns with too many canine teeth. This cruise ship was definitely made for nightlife.

Find Nina. That was the only clear objective in his mind, and somehow, he knew where she might be.

When the elevator doors rolled open on the sixtieth floor, Markham was the last still riding. He stepped out and squinted towards the canary dawn cutting diamonds across open ocean out the windows. The curtains were drawn apart. He moved in.

No one met his sight.

Markham was just about to admit his incorrectness when he saw her. His lips pressed together.

Nina sat cross-legged before the display of the Captain's handsome dark blue jacket, its long sleeves stiff and dignified as ever, lapels pressed and gold anchor buttons blindingly polished.

She jumped as Markham laid a hand on her shoulder.

"Hi," said Nina. She didn't look up.

"Hey," said Markham. He, too, gazed at the uniform.

Nina sighed.

"You . . ." Markham began.

"I just know he exists." She whispered. It broke his heart, and he hung his head. How could he say yes or no? Yes or no to a godlike figure who ran the ship Markham only boarded two days ago? He thought about the prose he'd read in *The Captain's Log* last night.

"This display . . ." Markham began. He was careful. "Maybe it's out here in the public's possession for a reason."

"Yes," Nina concurred fervently. "To remind us that he loves us."

Markham pursed his lips again.

"That's not what I was going to say. I was going to say . . . maybe it's here, for all of us, like a metaphor. That we chart our own courses. That we're all the captain of our souls."

There was a long pause. Markham realized his mistake.

Nina fell over the base of the display and sobbed. Markham crouched down next to her.

"I need him to exist." She covered her face, shaking. "To care . . ."

"I know he does," Markham said. A pang of guilt stabbed him for the lie. He pulled her arm down from her leaking eyes. She looked over at him. Despite what he felt inside, his face was resolute.

"Who couldn't care about you."

She dropped her head into him, and he wrapped his arms around her. Still crouched on his haunches.

His eyes were closed tight, his face to the side, but he surprised even himself with how confident his voice sounded.

"He cares about you."

NINE

The page creaked as Markham turned it.

"Shhhhh!"

Markham flinched. An unseen librarian had scolded him, and he looked around for her.

All the tomes here squawked upon opening. Every page in every book was plastic coated and waterproof. The blue shelves were like surrealist paintings, melting and dripping in fluidic shapes. To the right fluttered a fountain . . . of pages. A vacuum sucked the loose leaves from a basin, sorted them, and spit them back out in a constant stream of flapping paper.

Markham went back to his book.

It was titled *When Things Go Wrong: A Manual* and was written by an old First Mate who clenched a stubby pipe between his teeth and squinted in the black-and-white author photo on the back cover. Since it seemed like a companion to *The Captain's Log* (all copies of those were checked out), several red-spined copies lined the shelf. Markham sighed. They seemed worthless.

Something had changed after he held Nina like that and made a promise to her he didn't quite believe in. Yes, he still didn't want to be tried as a suspect in the First Mate's disappearance, and yes, he still needed to stick to the deal so Gavial would cover his rent. But now there was Nina and how he felt about her. Maybe if he found the First Mate, he could dry those tears on her cheeks.

He sent Nina to rest and told her he'd search the library for clues. They agreed to meet at the club later and discuss his findings over drinks.

Were the Captain's and the First Mate's disappearances prophesized? Did they ever imply where to find them should they go missing? Every answer he'd read in the *Manual* seemed metaphorical: ". . . in your heart," ". . . at the helm."

There was nothing.

Markham blinked crust from his eyes and tried to force the black smudges on the pages into words.

The selection of a First Mate is simple. Those desiring the position are invited to drop a letter into the mailbox located on the floor of the Captain's Parlor, addressed to "Helm: Room 1," with their own room number as the return address. If the current position holder is to die or be released, a new First Mate will be selected from the applicants within a matter of ten days and summoned in secret to the Captain's Quarters. Once ordained, they will then be revealed to the ship in proper uniform and may be verified by the tattoo on the back of their hand, given only by the Captain Himself and visible only when exposed to saltwater. They immediately reign as the new chief executive of the Mariners, whose authority in turn is exercised on the lay passengers, et cetera, et cetera.

So that answered the questions he hadn't thought to ask. First, the First Mate was a voluntary, albeit committed, position. And second, the ten days' time allotted to the selection of a new First Mate had well passed, eliminating the possibility of natural death or release. And confirming the suspicion that something was not right.

Markham dropped the book and ironed his eyelids with his wrists.

His watch rubbed him in the process, and he pulled back to look at it, surprised it was waterproof. Whoever he was in his forgotten past life, he must've been wealthy.

Late! Markham jolted out of the library chair and cringed at another "*Shhhh!*" from the spectral librarian. He looked up this time.

A female gargoyle with beaded glasses perched on one of the shelves, reading *The Old Woman and the Sea.*

Markham ducked out without risking an apology.

Bass-heavy techno music shook the floor and colors bounced off the walls. Markham bobbed his head in carefree enjoyment. He hadn't found Nina here yet but had accepted a green blended drink made from grass and palm leaves. Markham took a sip and squinted an eye in response.

It seemed like everyone was here, in this club hidden in the dank boroughs of the Mess. Abandoned alleys and battered dumpsters surrounded it. Markham had been shocked by its vibrancy when he stepped inside after looking cynically around the area.

Though the music was loud and skilled waiters artfully twirled around drinks and food to clusters of sitting clubbers, the mood seemed a little somber after the third no-show of the First Mate. Thoughtful conversation took place in pockets around the club. Brows were low, and headshaking occurred more frequently than nodding.

Markham tried not to notice. He downed his malty green drink.

When he opened his twitching eyes at last, he choked.

At the bar was Master Gavial, dressed in his buttoned white chef shirt and puffy grey pants. Claws crossed behind him, he bent his knees up and down to the music. His jaw was relaxed open. On top of his head, still as a statue, was one of his little hatchlings, also with its mouth open, showing its pointy baby teeth.

Markham tried to dislike Gavial for calling him a suspect, forcing him to work for his innocence. But something in his heart couldn't muster the anger. He wondered if Gavial saw him, and if he did, why he wasn't trying to keep a tighter leash on him when Nina wasn't around.

Next to Gavial, however . . .

Crocidius, a foot taller than Gavial, stood bipedal. For he had to. A bloody stump was far from healed where his right claw should be. His neck was craned down, mouth closed, but with teeth visibly snaking from his jaw. His vertical-slit pupils searched around the club.

So he didn't die.

. . . Good?

Markham tried to sneak away into a fold of people, but he couldn't ignore what happened next. Crocidius' eyes fell on him. He pushed Gavial and tossed his head towards Markham.

Gavial froze midsway with his knees bent. He registered Crocidius' meaning, darting his black eyes around once or twice. The lump at Crocidius' scaly tan throat bobbed, and Gavial shook his head in reply.

Crocidius seemed to frown. He took something from Gavial's shirt pocket and moved towards Markham. *Nowhere to run.* Markham reeled in breath and drew himself high.

The crocodile seemed even more nightmarish on two legs. Cracks ran through his brown scales as he walked. He stank like swamp and blood, so unlike Gavial's jasmine scent. Markham swallowed. Surely nothing would happen in public . . . around all these passengers . . .

Who all seemed to give Crocidius a wide berth.

With his gaze locked on Markham, Crocidius raised the item he'd taken from Gavial's pocket—a chalkboard with a whiteboard on the reverse—and used his nail to write something on the chalkboard side. The sound made Markham flinch. Crocidius turned the board towards Markham.

In wildly slanting letters, like palm trees bent in a hurricane, Crocidius had written *Where is she?*

Markham stared at it twice as long as it took to read it, stunned. And then he pulled a face like a teenager defying their parents.

"Nowhere you can get her," said Markham. He swung up his mixed drink only to find green dregs sliding along the glass.

Crocidius looked disgusted at Markham's stupidity. He

continued to stare, disapproving, as he rubbed out the chalkboard with his wrist. He wrote something else.

You're right.

"What?" blurted Markham. He froze.

Crocidius wiped out his board again and wrote. He turned it for Markham to see.

Because if she's not with you . . .

Wipe. Write. Show Markham.

Kloff's got her.

TEN

"Dagnabit, we've got to stop meeting like this, partner."

"Yee-haw."

Markham stared at Sylvester as Sylvester's lips wiggled in suppressed laughter.

"Stop," said Markham simply.

"I'm sorry," Sylvester screeched.

Gavial, arms crossed behind him, twisted on his feet towards the yodeling lone cowboy in the next room.

"Rodeo!" shouted Sylvester and then he clapped his hands over his own mouth.

"Yee-haw."

Markham gently slapped Sylvester. "Stop. That didn't even make sense."

Sylvester doubled over in laughter.

"Do we all understand what we're doing?" said Markham.

Sylvester nodded between tears of hilarity, and Gavial opened his mouth and breathed out seethingly like from an echoing cave.

"This is for Nina," Markham said. "Let's go."

They turned towards Kloff's graffitied door.

The dark room beyond was just as ominous as the first time Markham entered. Sylvester's shoes sifted through leaves of trash as he walked. Master Gavial strode in, bipedal, with unperturbed poise and confidence. And Markham whisked to the wall, into shadow. Unseen.

Markham flattened against the rough alley brick, sucking in his stomach. Fast his heart pattered, and he strained his neck to see around the bend of the wall. The bar of shadow from a lone streetlamp just cleared the tips of his boat shoes. In the burnt gas station still stood those two bullish monsters, gripping the revolving machine guns in front of them as before. One kicked its hoof and tossed its head again, but it only snorted and grunted in disappointment. *Master Gavial must be a figure they know they can't toy with.*

"Can I help you?" said the bored voice of the teenaged dark-skinned secretary at the desk. *Pop!* went the teenage girl's bubble-gum.

"Why, yes," said Sylvester.

Markham inched across the wall. He winced as chipped brick scraped loudly underfoot. But Sylvester commanded attention as he complained about the proximity of his and Gavial's rooms. Gavial held his head high with aplomb and ease.

At the bend of the wall, Markham bit his lip. He was about to enter the light of the streetlamp that led the way to that deserted, slum-like alley. Sylvester slammed the teenagers' desk.

"I want my money back for all the on-demand fruit dancers! The fruit was EXPIRED!"

Markham dove across the light and into the alley.

"ALL OF IT!" Another slam.

Graffiti bloomed and bubbled all over the walls that stretched ahead of Markham now for what seemed like miles. Kloff's name was everywhere, bathed in the orangish glow of the streetlamps. An alley cat furrowed into an arch and hissed at Markham.

"*Shhh!*" he scolded, glancing in the direction of the secretary desk. By the dramatized hollering of Sylvester, it seemed the kids had called upon the bulls to throw him out. Markham couldn't imagine such a horror but could visualize Gavial trailing calmly behind and then out the door. Surely, with his earned respect, they'd never touch him.

The black cat darted away into a pile of hood ornaments. After a few moments of fast walking, Sylvester's hollering faded into the distance. Anyone Markham ran into from this point on would assume the teenagers had let him in. He'd act cool. Speak to no one. Crocidius told him to meet him at Limbo, wherever that was.

How did Crocidius get into the place so easily?

Markham stuffed his hands in his pockets and traded his gait for one that shuffled and kicked. The walk was almost a half mile of reverberating silence. Shacks lined either side of the alley, built right on top of the sludge. Sewage pipes clunked and belched at the roofs. Tin barrels with radioactive warning signs glowed neon. Markham kept his head down. But the dwellings were not abandoned. Some human and some rat-like creatures lent him a cruel eye upon passing while they folded through trash piles or conversed with one another in what sounded like squeaks.

Still . . . as Markham scratched the side of his face to avert his gaze, he caught the worn misfortune on their faces, the hopelessness in their eyes.

Where had the Captain ever *been for them?*

He moved into louder, more populated ghetto—a fistfight down one alley, harsh laughter down another. A trolley of dynamite and coal barreled past. And then the ceiling opened up. It revealed levels and levels above like what could be seen from the grand glass elevator, except this was its mutant doppelgänger. Slime and rusticles hung off the balcony rails. Hundreds of holes spotted the levels like a giant ant colony.

No one paid him notice, but his breath quickened. *What is this place? What goes on here?* It was a whole other world, just like the Blue Star Line itself, but inverted.

Markham darted desperate eyes around for an inn or shop called Limbo, and then—a sign hung in the center of the street with an arrow pointing right.

Limbo →

Markham gulped.

He veered smoothly down the right alley. It was another tunnel with only one bend. Completely deserted. Not even a scrap of trash to scavenge, as if even the residents of this slum avoided this place.

Markham breathed in the foul air and moved forward. He turned the bend. This time only a few hundred feet awaited him. At the end, rungs embedded into a wall that led up to a hatch. A sign hung over this ladder with an arrow facing up.

Limbo ↑

He gripped the nearest metal rung. It was frozen, as if no living thing had touched it in years. Markham climbed up.

ELEVEN

What he found above the hatch made him gasp.

For the first time in days—and maybe forever, Markham didn't know—ocean breeze wafted over his silver hair.

The distant crash of waves against the keel tumbled in his ears. He rose onto the deck and kicked the hatch closed.

The deck was closed off with grates a few hundred yards behind him but ran forward into the distance for so long, it disappeared into fog. He shook his head in astonishment.

Trailing a hand along the rail, Markham checked out the ship exterior in the night for the first time. To his surprise . . . it was clean. Sharp. Well kept, well painted in bright white like a titanic yacht. Although the boards creaked under his feet, they were high-gloss teak. He swooped to look down over the deck—the breaking green waves were so far below they looked like tiny wriggles. It was as if he stood atop a skyscraper in the middle of the sea.

As far as Markham could tell from looking at the seemingly miles of empty deck, there was only one door—curved, metal, and framed with black-and-yellow hazard stripes. Watertight. He moved to it, overconfident with the exhilaratingly fresh salty breeze, and pulled on the handle.

Locked.

No matter. Crocidius said he'd meet him here—somehow. Markham turned away, rubbing his wrist, and leaned on the bulwark. He savored the view and the breeze. He felt amazing. Alive. Powerful. Free.

Hypnotically, the ropes fastening the hundreds of lifeboats below creaked back and forth . . . back and forth . . .

He closed his eyes. It was like a lullaby.

Twenty minutes passed. No one came. Markham slid to the floor, the bulwark at his back. An hour passed. Nothing.

He kneaded his eyes with his wrists. The crocodile had warned him of Nina's disappearance. He wouldn't have unless he was serious about helping find her . . . right?

Markham stood.

He cracked his neck. Paced around.

There was no going back. The deep sapphire night blushed with purple on the horizon. Oncoming dawn.

Markham scratched the back of his neck and looked each way on the deck. He stepped fast to the bulwark and loosened his belt. As if in accusation of what he was about to do, a line of tiny black frogs appeared out of nowhere and stared at him. He cursed and shooed them away with one hand, the other gripping the end of his belt. They hopped off and onto the deck.

He wrapped one hand around the shrouds hanging from

the upper deck and leaned forward, into the leeward wind. The shrouds creaked, and he parted his feet for balance, taking a swallow as the deck tossed beneath his shoes.

He released a trickle of urine. It grew from a shy stream to a strong, confident arc. His piss thudded hard against a lifeboat below—had this thing ever crashed? He casually stepped to the side. The hollow thudding ceased a few seconds later as his stream missed the target and disappeared into the air. He sighed in the warm breeze.

Then, behind him, the heavy door squawked open. He jumped, and a claw grabbed him.

TWELVE

The door boomed shut.

Markham sputtered and tripped forward as a brown claw pushed his shoulder hard.

Mildew decorated the floor like mustard-colored tie-dye. Ropes, nets, buoys, and torn red-and-white lifejackets crammed the hall.

"S-Sorry about back there," said Markham, "I just—"

Crocidius snarled, which most likely translated to *Shut up*.

Markham only nibbled the ground with his feet, afraid to tread on something sharp. The air reeked of aloe and rotten guacamole.

"Did you find her?" said Markham, voice darkening. "Is Kl—"

Crocidius' stump of an arm pinned him at the chest, and the intact brown claw covered Markham's face. His talons scraped down.

Markham cried out and crashed into a shelf of pool noodles. They *thwooped* to the floor by the dozens. He held his face. How stupid had he been for trusting the crocodile!

Crocidius snarled again, louder this time, and prodded him around a bend.

An open archway lay ahead with cells on either side. Markham planted a hand on the nearest wall, pushing himself back.

"Get off of me, you stupid animal." He thrust Crocidius away. "I won't give you the pleasure of delivering me to Kloff."

Crocidius lowered his snout, and his vertical slits stared into Markham for several long beats. Yet no aggression twisted his face. Instead, a line of intelligence probed behind his gaze. Markham's breath faltered as he studied the crocodile.

Then cackling laughter leapt into the air behind them. He spun.

Two loping, monkey-like beings apprehended his arms, their long limbs constricting him.

"Scram, Crocidy!" said the first. "We're taking the credit for this one!"

"Uncle Kloffy's going to love another bill!" The second laughed.

"Bills are his favorite," said the first.

Markham didn't remove his gaze from Crocidius as he stumbled backwards with the monkeys. Crocidius stood transfixed and didn't remove his gaze either.

"I don't have money," said Markham without hesitation.

"Not money bills," said one monkey, happily tugging him along.

"YOU are the bill," said the other.

"My name's not Bill."

The monkeys laughed.

Markham turned and walked straight under the archway with them.

The aloe-and-guacamole smell thickened. Large, sparse grains of sand more like pebbles just barely covered the floor. Markham grimaced as they crunched under his dock shoes.

To the side was a sagging brown surf bar, the straw of its hut so tan and old, the whole thing looked colorless. An oversized mortar and pestle full of brown mush was the source of the rotten guacamole. Potted palms and cacti surrounded the room. And in the center, between two unlit tiki torches . . .

The enormous blob that must have been Kloff sat on a white lifeguard-chair throne. His head lay back as two humans fanned him with palms. He groaned as if in pleasure, and his entire stomach rumbled visibly. The sound was like . . .

And that's when it hit Markham. Kloff and the Kloffers that looked like him . . .

Kloff belched black smoke.

They were all . . . literally volcanoes.

"Arr voo ai . . ." Kloff sang some ancient song. *"Key va te o . . ."*

As soon as Markham walked into the room, three human guards stationed at the walls in shadow gave a start. Eyes widened. Worried looks were exchanged. They squeezed their tridents. Markham was sure he heard one of them—a trench coat-wearing man—gulp.

Kloff hadn't yet looked down.

"Eayerrr iii . . ."

"Uncle Klofffffyyy!" one of the monkeys hooted.

"Gur te voo," sang Kloff.

"UNCLE KLOFFY, UNCLE KLOFFY!" The other one jumped up and down. They stopped Markham right before him.

"Grrrrrr rrrrr . . ."

Were those lyrics, too?

"WE FOUND YOU ANOTHER BILL AND HE'S GAVIAL'S FRIEND!"

"*And cross our paths again,*" Kloff dropped his great head at last and sang the final words in a tongue Markham could understand.

The volcano-man's ugly face froze.

Markham's arm muscles tightened in fear. Silence fell upon the entire room. And then the monkeys danced around him.

"Uncle Kloffy happy with our catch?" said one.

"If not, we eat him, maybe?" said the other, leaping up recurrently like an excited piranha.

"What the hell?" Markham looked down at their skipping.

Kloff drew a gun from his side and fired.

The monkeys screamed and bolted off, and Markham turned around.

The man in the trench coat lay dead at the wall. His trident clamored to the ground, and blood pooled beneath him.

"Now . . ." Kloff's voice rumbled as if getting ready to erupt. He seethed, emitting more smoke.

"What do you want, you unfortunate piece of scum?"

Markham swallowed, recovering from the murder he had just witnessed.

"I want Nina. Now."

Kloff laughed so loudly the pots rattled on the floor. Then Markham's eyes widened in horror as lava dripped like spittle from Kloff's mouth. It singed his skin and hardened into rock that crumbled off him.

"You are a barnacle that clings to this ship. Why would your demands mean anything to me? First you sneak onto my deck, then you—"

"Your henchman tricked me."

"Mmm . . ." Kloff contemplated, not bothering to ask which henchman.

Markham wiped off some blood that had dripped from his cuts onto his lip. He studied the mob lord as the mob lord studied him. Then Markham's eyes narrowed. There was something artificial behind the way Kloff looked at him. Kloff seemed to be trying too hard to hastily reinforce the indifference in his eyes.

"What . . . is your name?" he asked.

"Markham Brody."

Kloff's eyes relaxed then. Markham didn't fail to notice the reaction.

"Markham Brody," Kloff repeated.

"Yeah. Now where is Nina? I'm sure Gavial won't tolerate—"

"You are my next bill, Markham Brody."

"What?"

"I do not deal with money like my dirty rival, Obensteen. His Helmsman, the Captain, wouldn't approve. To him . . . lives are what speaks. So, lives are my bills. When I have enough captured, I will convince him to come out and play."

Shock jolted through Markham. "The Captain. You—are you hiding the Captain?!"

Smoke snaked through Kloff's teeth. He tried not to laugh.

"No. I do not need to."

Hands grabbed Markham—the other, still-living guards.

"The cells are full, lord. Where should we throw him? Overboard?"

"No," said Kloff. He tilted his head, and his voice filled with playful conspiracy. "Put him in . . . 88B."

"Yes, m'lord."

They hauled him backwards until Markham's heels dragged.

"TELL ME WHERE SHE IS!" Markham shouted. "I'LL KILL YOU, KLOFF!"

But even he knew the words were a lie.

Back in the prison hall, Crocidius was no longer there. But Markham's questions faded as he grunted and jerked to avoid the painful punches of the guards, who beat him before unlocking his cell.

They tossed him inside and slammed the door. The locks jingled once again.

It was dark but not black. Markham hauled himself to a stand.

Another figure was curled in the fetal position in the corner. For one hopeful moment, he thought it was Nina; the prisoner was so thin. And then the prisoner turned over.

His eyes were white and bright in contrast to the dimness of the cell. They soldered into Markham.

Markham breathed heavily, sizing the other up: friend or foe?

The other rose and took two tentative steps towards Markham.

Markham took one back.

Closer, Markham could see the man was middle-aged with black hair flecked with grey, his eyes like frigid oceans speckled with glaciers. He wore a white jacket . . . silver buttons and epaulettes accenting the uniform . . .

Markham's breath caught. He knew who stood before him.

First Mate Yastley.

"Oh . . . my . . . g—"

The First Mate lunged and rammed Markham against the wall.

Markham's skull banged against metal.

The First Mate looked unhinged, his eyes swiveling over Markham. His hot breath blew over Markham's neck. His hands trembled with strength and insanity as they gripped Markham's shirt hard.

Markham gurgled against the wall and strained to look down, coughing out blood and spit.

The First Mate spoke in a wheeze.

"*You.*"

PART TWO:

THE HELM

THIRTEEN

The First Mate's hands continued to shake, but no longer from anger. Now he sobbed. He fell to his knees and dragged Markham over.

Damn . . . thought Markham. *Maybe I did try to kill this guy . . .*

"All right." Markham coughed. "All right." He shimmied Yastley off his leg and sidestepped away.

Yastley curled into himself again and chanted. *"You . . . you . . . you . . ."*

"Yeah," Markham breathed, looking around for a weapon. "Me . . . me . . . me . . ."

"I love you," Yastley gasped.

"I love you, too," Markham replied automatically, still scanning around for a blunt object.

"Here," Yastley muttered. *"You're here . . ."*

Markham picked up a broken, rotten paddle from the floor. "Right here." He squeezed the paddle, lifted it over his head, then stopped.

This shriveled-up little man mumbled and shook.

Markham lowered the paddle and sighed.

The First Mate continued to mutter words of affection at Markham. Not exactly things one would say to a person who tried to kill them.

And then a spot of color caught Markham's eye.

A photograph lay on the floor where Yastley had originally been sleeping. Markham glanced at Yastley once more and then went to retrieve it.

Mildew crusted the white border of the Polaroid shot. The colors were outdated and dull. Light splotched parts of Yastley's face. But none of it was enough to mistake the bruises, cuts, and stains of blood muddying his skin.

In the picture, Yastley sat with his back to the tiki bar. Unconscious. Head lolled. His limp hand held a white sign.

Salute the "K"aptain.

Horrified, Markham's mouth dropped.

For the next hour, Markham sat against the wall, holding the photo in one hand, paddle in the other. Staring at Yastley and thinking hard. Yastley did not stop his murmuring and hiccupping until at last he droned off into what might have been sleep.

Markham twirled the paddle on the ground again and again. It clapped against the wood floor.

The locks at the cell door jingled. Markham slapped the paddle still and stiffened.

A Polaroid camera was the first and only thing he saw in the doorway. Dark laughter accompanied it.

Markham scrambled back into the wall as far and for as long as he could until the gangsters' hands became too firm and too many.

Pain sprang through Markham's jaw and turned his face sideways. He spat out blood as if it were seawater and ran his tongue along his teeth. None uprooted yet. Somewhere, he heard a fresh pair of knuckles crack in preparation.

Another punch sent his head forward again. His vision rocked in and out like a buoy in a storm, but he didn't have the strength or interest to lift his gaze to his offenders.

The snakelike lens of the Polaroid probed into his face. One of Kloff's men with pointy black nails held the device.

Markham was against the tiki bar, just as Yastley had been. A Salute the "K"aptain sign like Yastley had held perched in Markham's lap. Kloff was absent from his lifeguard-chair throne, and the expired guacamole behind Markham thickened the air. Photo shoot umbrellas and bulbs stood around him, black and mocking like twisted peacocks.

"Why?" Markham managed to croak, blinking as his face swelled.

"Becauuuuuuuse!" the crony replied. "The camera loves you!"

"Now pass out already," a second, deeper voice added—the one that had cracked his knuckles. His cohort chuckled.

"Why *me?*" Markham used all his energy. "No one will care . . . what I think of Kloff." He swallowed.

"Why's that, oyster head?" said the cameraman.

"I just boarded."

Whack!

Markham yelled out.

"Kloff's orders. It don't matter how popular you are," the deep voice responded, and all Markham saw was him rubbing his fist. "All that matters is that the passengers see their fellows falling one by one . . ."

Whack!

"And no Captain caring enough to stop it," said the cameraman. His fingers drummed the lens impatiently.

WHACK!

Markham choked at that last hit. His vision blurred and didn't refocus. Not in three seconds . . . five . . .

Wait. There. Just a little. Just enough to see . . .

Crocidius stood there like a towering sculpture. In his brown claw was another sign, stick-like letters scratched out with his nail.

Stay conscious. Buy me time.

His black vertical eyes drilled into Markham, even from afar. Markham blinked.

"Wha's the matter with you?!" said the cameraman. "Just knock him out, you idiot!"

The deep-voiced gangster growled in offense and determination. "He don't wanna be out-knocked!"

The next blow toppled Markham over. He landed on one outstretched arm and turned his head against the sticky skin of his inner elbow. Blood ran from his nose like rainwater from the gutter. The gangsters laughed. Markham stayed conscious.

"Again," said the cameraman.

Less and less vision returned after each punch.

Stay conscious.

Stay conscious.

His breath came in—

Was it coming at all?

He lifted a hand to his face to see if he could still feel it. He stuffed his fingers into his mouth, onto the wet bed of his tongue. He no longer opened his eyes, but he was there.

"One more should—Wh-Wha—?!"

The gangsters screamed. With every effort, Markham split open his eyes.

Crocidius' Jurassic claw and stump knocked the heads of the two cronies together. The Polaroid dropped and cracked, flashing off one last photo. And behind Crocidius—

"Markham!" Nina dove for his bloody lump of a body. A whisper into his ear. "I knew you'd come. But look at you . . ."

Crocidius growled in impatience.

"Come on," said Nina. She tried to pull Markham to his feet, but he was dead weight. Crocidius pushed Nina aside and fell to his stomach.

Markham felt a jaw slide beneath him. Hot, rancid breath washed over him. A rumble like thunder bowled from the bowels of the crocodile's throat.

And that was the last thing he saw.

FOURTEEN

Ice crinkled in the bag as Nina pressed it against Markham's head. Markham closed his eyes, allowing the frigid moisture to numb his skin. Pain throbbed in his skull thanks to all that banging against the floor every time Crocidius had thumped onto his stub.

"Poor Markham," Nina whimpered. She leaned against his chest as he stood at the wall. Her face turned to the sound of his heartbeat, so close she could hear him swallow. "You're still shaking."

"Kloff's a psychopath." Markham's voice caught. He cleared it fast.

"*Hrrrrmph! Rrrmph!*" Crocidius tore through bags of frozen food. Cool air wafted against them.

They were sheltering in a dark, cluttered refrigerator. Lint, feathers, and tartar sauce stuck to the crocodile's scales from the torn sacks, making him look like a monstrous piñata. With his one good claw, he pressed against the wall, a hunk of frost-coated orca blubber between his jaws and eyes blank with animalistic occupation. He seemed to struggle with the blubber as if it were alive, concentrating every muscle, and then he jerked into a barrel roll. The meat tore, and he chugged it down in several gulps.

"I know," Nina said. "He's the one who took my finger."

"Why did he take you this time?" Markham winced against the ice.

"*Shh*—please." Nina grasped him tighter.

"Why did he take you?" he demanded harder.

"Markham." She shushed him again.

Markham looked up and around. Confused. "Where are we?"

Crocidius chirped out a craggy, grizzled sound. His black slit eyes lurked over to Nina.

"We brought you through the vent before the guards came to," she translated. "But we're not down to the lower decks yet. We're still in Kloff's turf."

"How do we get back?"

Crocidius opened his jaw and snarled. Saliva threaded between his upper and lower teeth.

"He doesn't know a way without being caught. He's doing the best he can."

"Seriously, how did you get all of that from a growl?" said Markham. An uncomfortable pause followed. Crocidius' blank orbs stared at him awkwardly. There was a single click in the back of his throat.

"Well?" Markham raised his eyebrows at Nina. "Now what did he say?"

"He actually didn't say anything that time."

Markham bumped his head back against the wall and gazed up at the ceiling.

Then something rustled beside him. He jumped.

"AH!" Markham's cry was pitched higher than he'd hoped. Nina kept a supportive hand on his shoulder.

First Mate Yastley stood up from stealing a tin of caviar from a cooler. He chewed with vigor and stared unwaveringly at Markham.

"What's he doing here?" Markham was breathless.

"He's—Markham, this is the First Mate!" Nina broke out a winded smile. "It's the First Mate, Markham! Didn't you recognize him in your cell?"

"Yeah," said Markham. "And he tried to kill me."

"He's a little traumatized," Nina equipped.

"You think I might have actually . . . tried to kill him in the past?" Markham thought back to Gavial and Nina apprehending him as a suspect in the pillow room.

"No." Nina scoffed. "He's been trying to ask us if you're okay over and over. He's not scared of you."

"Why is he still looking at me like that?" said Markham. Yastley shoved more caviar in his mouth and continued to stare fiercely.

"He's . . ." Nina, still holding Markham's shoulder, turned to observe Yastley. "He . . . likes you?"

She waved a hand in front of Yastley's eyes. The First Mate didn't blink. Continued to chew.

"Look, there's no way we were leaving the *First Mate*, Markham! We *found* him! And maybe with a little . . . *therapy*, he can tell us where the Cap—"

Yastley dropped the tin and lunged for Markham.

Crocidius roared like a lion, and Yastley sprang back. His upper lip twitched. Everyone looked at each other.

"What did he say that time?" Markham finally squeaked.

Nina swallowed. "He didn't. He roared."

Markham buried his face in his hands.

"All right, look," said Nina. "We have to get out of here. Kloff will know we're all gone by now."

Markham rolled out his sore shoulders and carefully stepped from the wall towards the door near Crocidius. Nina held his shoulder with both hands and walked with him.

"Once we get back, what's to stop Kloff from taking us again in our sleep?" Markham watched the chips of ice on the floor with caution as he walked.

"We'll figure that out when we *do* get back, Twenty-Six." Nina looked at Crocidius for approval before she reached for the door. He didn't object. She pushed it open.

Markham looked over his shoulder at Yastley once before leaving with her.

Behind her, Crocidius grunted directions. They crept through unlit halls. Plain wooden passages. Inflatable lifeboats that seemed half a century old were stuffed in overhead compartments, their dirtied white strings hanging down in the cramped halls. Nina fiddled her fingers together.

"Is this right?" she asked, voice low.

Crocidius hummed ominously. Markham looked sideways at Nina. She returned the gaze and hesitated.

"He doesn't know anymore."

Markham continued to move stiffly.

A pair of eyes passed him. He looked over.

The first accent in what felt like miles, an oil portrait framed in chipped gold hung on the wall. It depicted an old dark-skinned First Mate with a wooly black beard and reddish nose. Everyone glanced at it, their expressions a little more wary and thoughtful as they moved past.

Another portrait hung on the left. This one had an intentionally weathered driftwood frame. This former First Mate, painted in dreamier, impressionistic pastels, wore a bandana over his eyes and a stern expression—he was blind. The silver buttons on his white jacket seemed to reflect the dark navy, almost black, coat of a man standing at the easel . . .

"Crocidius . . ." Nina's voice was close to fear.

They passed several more portraits. Yastley's murmurings grew louder behind them. He wrung his hands repeatedly.

Finally, ahead, a familiar face outlined in a new, pristine black frame stared back at them. A photograph rather than a painting.

Yastley. Smiling. Healthy and bright. Teeth straight. He looked as friendly and ordinary as a soccer coach posing for a yearbook.

They stopped.

Yastley shouldered past them, in a trance.

He approached his portrait and stared at it. The others' reflections in the glass moved closer after him.

And then Yastley turned to the door on the next wall.

The door had rounded corners. A polished mahogany helm's wheel was mounted in its center. Gold bordered the doorframe, etched with nautical pictograms—seagulls, mermaids, narwhals, and porpoises—and mother-of-pearl tile shone like a doormat at its bottom.

A platinum plaque with laser engraving hung over the door.

Captain's Quarters.

FIFTEEN

"Markham, it's him!" Nina gasp-laughed and streaked for the door. Her face was childlike as she ran her hands over every spoke of the wheel at the door. She shook her head, tucked back a strand of hair, and swallowed. Her eyes glimmered.

Markham, mouth open, approached slowly.

"Nina, this—"

Yastley shoved him forward from behind, and Markham stumbled.

"Hey! Watch it, you foaming—!"

Crocidius emitted a half hiss, half roar. Nina was starting to turn the wheel. He lunged in front of her on his stomach like a torpedo, and Nina staggered back and tripped. Markham caught her under the arms with both hands and looked up, breathless. The reptile's jaw stayed poised open, his eyes a blank fixture.

"He better be saying something," said Markham. Neither he nor Nina attempted to stand her back up yet.

"Crocidius?" said Nina.

Crocidius made a clucking sound. He remained frozen in his openmouthed vacuity.

Nina blinked. She seemed to consider his words.

"He says we should have a guard wait outside before we go in."

"Guard?" said Markham. "Go in? Isn't it locked?"

"Oddly . . . no," said Nina, as if just realizing how that might be concerning.

Crocidius clucked once more as if this proved his point. Nina straightened from Markham's hold and brushed herself off.

"All right," she said. "Well, since Yastley's already met him, he can keep—"

Crocidius snarled.

"What?" Nina challenged. "No. He has to meet him, too."

"What's he saying?" said Markham.

"He says *you* should keep watch outside," said Nina.

"No!" echoed Markham, and at the same time—

"NO!" shouted Yastley. Everyone turned to him. It was the first he'd spoken since the refrigerator. A long, confounded pause followed.

"I want to go in," Markham finally declared. He took a step towards the door.

And Crocidius rose onto his lower legs. Slowly he grew to his towering height and overshadowed Markham's smaller figure. The crocodile's eyes bore into him threateningly.

Something instinctive burned through Markham's stomach: old fear and intuition. He remembered the first moment he'd met the powerful brown swamp monster, the hostile distrust in

Crocidius' eyes compared to the genial brightness of his green cousin's. The claws digging protectively into Master Gavial's shoulders . . .

Crocidius had never been on Markham's side.

. . . Had he?

Crocidius had never explained his reason for mauling Markham's face earlier, never explained his chewing of Markham's leg.

But he'd indeed saved Nina. And he didn't push Markham overboard on the deck when he'd had the chance.

But why would Crocidius not want him to enter the Captain's chamber?

Markham lunged for the door around Crocidius and forced it open.

He would find out.

SIXTEEN

"Wait!" Nina shouted behind Markham.

It seemed she didn't mean to stop him like Crocidius had—only that she didn't want him to enter without her.

Markham felt his foot snag as he delved inside. He spun and hobbled backwards into the cabin on one foot, looking down at the strange white sheet that entangled him.

Nina rushed in. Markham froze with his wrapped foot still off the ground. He raised his eyebrows at her and turned to the room at large.

The Captain's Quarters were wrecked.

Oil lamps lay broken on their sides. Anchor-print wallpaper curled down to reveal wooden framework. Fiji water bottles lay empty next to expensive antique navigational instruments on desks—a jumbled collage of parchment and brass that bounced off every reflection of chaos in the chamber. A fathometer in the corner scratched out measurements for canyon and ocean depths on white graph paper like a lie detector, though it seemed to beep its last breaths with dying power.

Only two features of the room remained intact.

The first was the king-sized four-poster bed trimmed in antique gold and covered by a deep-blue blanket. Over it, like the bonnet of a crib, was an authentic Megalodon jaw at least eight feet tall. Hand-sized teeth arched over the mattress like a demented rainbow of light and dark grey. Not a tooth was missing.

The second was the coffee-table-sized basin in the center of the room holding the red and black arrows of a giant compass encased in cocobolo wood. The compass' convex glass cover was unscathed.

Markham freed his foot.

"Oh my god," he said.

The excitement and wonder disappeared from Nina's face. Her eyes were blank but for disbelief.

Yastley wandered in behind them. Instead of having another nervous breakdown as Markham expected, the First Mate moved forward, mouth wilted in a frown. He paused, then slowly picked up a page from the floor and looked down at it for a long time.

Crocidius, probably due to whatever reasons he'd had against them all entering, hung broodingly in the doorway and glared in.

"What happened here?" Markham drifted forward.

The floorboards creaked. He looked down as his shoes pressed against the ground. Dark blood soaked deep into the wood. He pulled his foot back fast.

"There's blood."

"Where is he." Nina's voice was too desperately flat. Markham looked over at her.

"There's *blood*," he repeated, as if this should explain something.

"Where *is he?!*" Nina tore farther into the chamber. She heaved open a pair of tall closet doors and began digging.

"Nina!" Markham barked. Annoyed. What happened here was clear.

"What happened to him?!" Her voice rose an octave from inside the closet.

Markham sat on the Captain's crisp, empty bed. He sighed and touched a hand to his mussed grey hair, looking around in calm understanding. He'd just have to wait it out until Nina realized it too.

Crocidius crept in on his stomach. His eyes darted around, wary.

When Nina's charades went on too long, Markham spoke. "Yastley."

Yastley snapped towards Markham. His eyes were alert and his back straightened. Markham didn't register it, still dazing off at a corner of the destroyed chamber.

"Tell Nina the Captain's been kidnapped or murdered."

"SHUT *UP*, MARKHAM!" Nina yelled.

"You know what happened to him, Yastley," said Markham. "Speak. Tell her."

Tears filled Yastley's eyes. A battle waged over his features—to articulate or not to articulate? His fingers—still battling a better will—crawled up to embrace his arms, and he sunk to the floor.

Markham lifted a hand in the First Mate's direction, then slapped it back to his knee. "Does that confirm it for you, Nina?"

"No," said Nina. She threw a pair of the Captain's polished black dress shoes at him, and they toppled over the floor.

"For me?" Markham said sarcastically. "Thanks." He reeled

them closer. They looked sturdier and less beaten-up than his brown boat shoes. He untied one shoe and exchanged a foot.

It slipped right in. Comfortable as ever.

Markham raised his eyebrows. "That was convenient." He put on the other and lifted the boat shoes in one hand, then stood.

His voice dropped tenderly. "We need to get back to the lower decks, dear." He still looked around, calmly determined that he was right. "He's not here."

Nina emerged from the closet. Her clothes, hair, and expression were ruffled.

Markham, still holding his old shoes in one hand, moved to her. He pressed his free hand firmly to the back of her head, forcing her to come to him. Come against him.

She did.

His voice was a whisper only she could hear.

"But I'm here."

In front of Yastley and Crocidius, Markham stooped to her mouth and swept his lips against hers gently. His hands came up to grasp her face, the rubbery soles of the docksiders touching her ear.

A disgusted, impatient sound ripped from Crocidius, and he thrashed his tail at a broken vase. Naturally, this frightened off a cluster of black frogs who had appeared to watch.

Crocidius tromped on his stump back over to the door, careful not to cut himself on any severed glass.

Markham pulled back. "He's right."

"You understood him?" Nina said.

A half smile cocked Markham's mouth. "Didn't have to."

"Wait," she said. Markham, already making for the door, turned back to her.

"We don't have a camera. I need to remember this place."

"Mental photographs?" Markham suggested.

"No." Nina shook her head. Markham resisted rolling his eyes and stood still as he watched her go to the Captain's desk. She shuffled out a drawer and rifled around for a pen. "I'll draw it."

A fountain pen with a fine point emerged in her intact, five-fingered hand.

She sifted through astronomical charts and illegible documents on sea creatures for a spare piece of paper.

Markham stepped closer, curious.

Nina stopped when her hand fell on a page. She froze.

Blood stained the paper.

She whipped it out from the others.

Red splattered the page so gruesomely that Nina's skin faded a shade lighter.

And when she read it, she did more than gasp. She dropped the pen and her hand leapt to her mouth.

Yastley looked up from the floor in renewed arousal. Crocidius, possibly more ghoulish looking than ever—demonic purplish hollows around his slit eyes—crawled towards the desk.

Nina dropped the page and staggered backwards, hand still over her mouth, skin as white as sails. She almost fell.

Markham's adrenaline sprung through him, and he caught her and actually shouted.

"What?!" he yelled. "What?!"

Nina turned to him so abruptly, and with eyes so wide in shock, fear, and—Markham pulled an astounded expression—*awe* that he let her go.

One single beat followed.

And then Nina retrieved the paper and pulled her hand down from her mouth.

"Sign your name on a page." Her voice seemed to belong to someone else. She pointed at the desk and the pen.

Markham followed her finger. To end this terrifying uncertainty, he obliged the bizarrely timed instruction.

He took the pen and signed his name in a fast, instinctive motion.

Nina snatched it almost before he lifted the pen.

She looked at the two papers in her hands.

And then . . .

With a dazed, numb face, she turned both the blood-stained leaf and the new signature page to him.

The signatures matched.

SEVENTEEN

"STOOOOOOOOP!!!!" Markham banged the Captain's desk with one of the brass sextants. *"I'M NOT THE CAPTAIN!"*

Crocidius was attacking Yastley, who was lunging for Markham, who was pushing away a blubbering Nina with one hand.

"I'M NOT THE CAPTAIN!" Markham yelled again. Everyone stopped mid-claw/lunge/blubber. Markham looked around at the frozen silence. "Although I do have remarkable vocal authority."

"But—" Nina began.

And then the floors, walls, and all the wood in between began to screech. The ground lurched, and everyone but Crocidius reached out for support.

Crocidius plunged forward and rammed Nina in the shins so she'd collapse on top of him. With a cry, she grasped the great reptile's body, and Crocidius bolted for the door as knickknacks thundered down from surfaces.

Markham and Yastley ran after them, stumbling as the angle of the floor increased in severity.

Someone was turning the ship. Hard.

"FOLLOW HIM!" Nina cried. Yastley and Markham chased after Crocidius as he traversed the musky narrow halls. Markham shoved Yastley aside once as the First Mate, grinning, tried to plant a kiss on his cheek.

Behind them, orange-and-white lifeboats fell off the overhead shelves and thumped to the ground.

Markham caught the tough rope. He flicked away the seaweed hanging off it and tied it to the balcony post. The aardvark-looking being that threw it to him gave the "okay" gesture and lumbered off to tie his end on the other side. Seaweed hung off him like a shawl.

Immediately passengers lined up to use the rope, which had cones like buoys at intervals. The *floof!* and *whap!* of more ropes being thrown and fastened on all decks could be heard. The deep rumble of an object rolling down slopes was still frequent.

The ship did not right itself after that initial lurch in the hour it took for Crocidius to lead Markham, Nina, and Yastley back to the main areas. Every floor remained frozen in at least a thirty-degree angle. Passengers were establishing extra supports and lifelines—like the ropes—and the ruckus was high and shrill. They'd been in a sharp, unending turn all day.

"This has never happened! Never!" a man yelled while tugging himself up the rope to the elevator.

"No Captain of mine steers like this!" another replied, shuffling down far too fast.

"Exactly," someone added. "Because he's not steering us no more!"

"Did you see the First Mate? Did you see what they done to him?"

When the public had spotted Yastley, they swarmed him. He looked like the First Mate they all remembered, but he was so deranged and gaunt that a saltwater-drinking passenger immediately conducted the authenticity test, pouring seawater on Yastley's hand. The First Mate's official, Captain-given tattoo of an anchor and rope appeared on his skin to the gasps of those around them. Crocidius snuck away on his belly between anxious feet, and Nina dragged Markham aside as he tried to watch.

"Careful with him!" Markham had yelled. No one cared that he'd recovered the First Mate—not when the First Mate was present. "He's sick!"

They'd figured that out quickly on their own, along with Yastley's lost speech capability, and ushered him away with loving reverence into the hands of professional-looking physicians and well-timed reporters.

"Markham, listen to me," Nina said, pressing against him in a way that seemed a little unintentional by the angle in the corner. She kept her breathless voice low. Her eyes swam with tears that looked joyful as she grasped his shoulders. "You're the Captain."

Markham replied a beat later, as if he hadn't heard. "What?" He sort of hadn't.

"You're the *Captain*," she whispered again, sounding half-elated, half-disbelieving.

"I'm not the Captain." Firm.

"You *are*, Markham."

"No!" He shook her shoulders back. "Just like I wasn't a Kloffer, either. Why can't you accept that I'm just *some guy*."

"Because you're not." Nina tried to lift a hand to Markham's cheek, but he pulled away.

"You're right. How cliché of me—because *some guy* is always the chosen one, right?"

Nina blinked.

"So, I'm not *some guy*; I'm Markham Brody, and I was stupid enough to fall into the water somewhere and almost end up as half a fish n' chips."

Nina rolled her eyes. "So, if you're not a Kloffer, not the Captain, why would you have been wearing that Kloff shirt? Huh?" She jostled him. "It all makes *sense*, Markham. They put it on you before you went overboard."

"*Or!* Crazy thought! I was homeless on this ship, picked my clothes from garbage cans, got drunk, and accidentally tumbled over." Markham's voice was shaking with heat. "I'm not gonna lie, Nina, sounds a lot more like me."

"And the signature matching? Are you serious?"

Markham shrugged. "Abducted and framed doesn't seem out of the question, either."

Nina tightened her grasp of him. "You're denying it because you don't want it to be true."

"And you're making it true because you want it to be."

Nina's face reddened. She had no reply.

"If I'm the Captain," Markham pointed in the direction of the elevator, "let's march right up to the Captain's Parlor and rip that sand dollar off the uniformed mannequin. Didn't you say it'll burn me if it doesn't belong to me?"

"No, the Captain's would almost kill you."

"But I'm the Captain, so let's go."

"No," said Nina.

"You don't sound so confident anymore when I put it like that."

"No, Markham, you don't need to test it on the stupid sand dollar." Nina's voice begged. "I believe it *wouldn't* kill you. Because you're the Captain." Impatience touched her timbre. Then her volume rose with frustration. "You ARE the—"

"NINA," Markham barked. He shoved down her hands. "I'm NOT." His blue eyes flashed.

She stared at him. A long, anguished beat followed.

And then she darted away, wobbling down the fun house angles.

"Where are you going?!" he shouted after her.

"Well, *someone* has to be!" she retorted with anger, and soon the bodies of anxious passengers drowned her from view.

Markham sighed. He rubbed his face, then got to work helping passengers with the ropes.

The bustle continued through the night. Markham hung over the balcony on the forty-third floor and laid his head on the rail in exhaustion. His feet gave way, and he sank to his knees.

He stayed there until the deep, lazy bells tolled for breakfast.

By the third day of endless turning, passengers were not as inquiring and eager to adapt. The betting games of rolling lifesavers down the halls and resounding high fives as one tumbled faster than the others had died. *The Blue Star News* staff had printed and distributed a paper with lines of diagonal writing and cutoff words. Its front page reported the recovery of First Mate Yastley, and that his incapacity and obvious torture yielded no answers to the Captain's absence or the Great Turn, as it had already been christened. "Doctors report intense mental and physical torture of our beloved First Mate Yastley, who is still unable to commune on the fate of the Captain, but psychological experts say he seems to be showing signs of inexpressible knowledge," the article wrote. "Who is taking over our ship?"

Nina had disappeared as effectively as the First Mate had done. When Markham went looking for her in the galley, he found Master Gavial wearing pink earmuffs. Gavial had ordered the temperature in his kitchen to drop to a shiver because coolness helped neutralize the effects of nausea. He valiantly directed his staff with a raised claw and deft bipedal pacing through the white-tiled aisles. Cooks had to hold their pots by hand with mittens as the water boiled and flames leapt in all the wrong directions. A lobster rolled down the halls between the stainless-steel appliances flapping its claws more than once.

But Nina was not there.

By day five of the Great Turn, spirits broke. Passengers slumped and slugged against the supports, the smell of vomit no longer lifted with soap and mop. Water from the spilled sauna pool leaked through the doors and dribbled down the balcony onto the dining parlor at the bottom. Master Gavial had stood in the center and raised his oblong snout to the dripping of hot, stewy water. He frowned.

Markham lay in bed with his hands over his eyes. His stomach churned. His shoulder pressed against the wall that his bed had slid into.

And then the long, low belch of the ship's horn blasted through the walls of his cabin and vibrated the bedstead.

Everyone stumbled out of their holes and nests and drunken

stupors to the common areas around the balconies of the elevator. They looked around, as dumbfounded as Markham.

The elevator, a common focal point to hundreds of onlookers on the sixty floors, was moving.

It stopped on every level and opened its doors. The *ding* was constant, perfectly timed, and eerie. On each floor, a rush of fluttering paper followed the sound, as if someone were opening the door of a library in the middle of a tornado and then closing it.

When the lift dinged and opened on Markham's floor, a gargoyle-like minion, crouched and cackling, shoved out a bag of fliers. Black bags stuffed with paper were stacked within the elevator as if it were a mail room.

Many gathered with Markham to pick up a flyer.

Markham recognized the picture on it.

First Mate Yastley, unconscious, beaten, holding the SALUTE THE "K"APTAIN sign.

The message came on laughable but entirely unfunny Kloff letterhead.

IF UR CAPTAIN LIVED, HE'D STEER U STRAIT

I IS UR "K"APTAIN

EIGHTEEN

The sweet smell of piña coladas and margaritas rose through the air. Churning water roared far down below the decks, and the ship rocked with its ever-circling direction. Markham sighed and half walked, half tripped into the bamboo lounge chair roasting in the afternoon sun. He tripped almost everywhere he went now.

On the way to this little outdoor cabana, he'd wandered deep into the recesses of the thirty-first floor, past shops barred by Closed signs and sad, queasy store owners sweeping up broken seashells; bottles of honey-colored boat oil; and essence-of-kiwi-and-mango tanning balm that had fallen from shelves. Passengers skirted away from the main hallways as more and more of Kloff's gnarly minions lurked against the walls and loped into the alleys with bags of his fliers. Markham just followed the painted signs of piña coladas—white slushies in curvy glasses.

Now, he squinted and flattened the wrinkled paper in his hand—the same paper that was in the hands of almost everyone around him.

The flier from Kloff. Many wept over it. Many dropped their mouths and raised their heads, aghast. Markham just sighed again.

So Kloff was taking over the ship. How bad could that be, when the only alternative was to pretend that *he* was the Captain? The true Captain was dead. The destroyed cabin proved it. And that signature in the Captain's Quarters, that evidence Nina had taken for fact, must have been no more than another plant by Kloff's campaign, just like Markham had said. What surer failure could there be against Kloff than to frame a clueless week-old passenger, such as Markham, as the almighty figure at the helm? Given that Markham arrived on the ship wearing a Kloff shirt, it made sense the Kloffers would keep trying to set him up.

The back of the flier contained further instructions.

Until yous all submit yous sand dollar amulets to the new "K"aptain through the mailbox in the "K"aptain's Parlor as if yous were applying for the First Mate—Helm: Room 1—the ship will continue to turn!!!! . . .

Exclamation points took up three more lines of text.

. . . Wroten support example to include with amulet:

"I salute the "K"aptain!"

- Kloff

An image of a smoking volcano appeared below his name.

Markham rolled his eyes and tucked the flier back in his pocket.

Nina hadn't come to see him in nearly a week. He'd spotted her only at a distance as she handed out bowls of kelp noodle soup to the queasy, who waited outside Gavial's kitchen like stray puppies. On another occasion, he halted when he saw her several yards down the deck. She was flipping a sea turtle back onto its belly after the Great Turn had tilted it over. Nina had walked away as the turtle took a few steps and then promptly keeled over again. That time she heaved a great sigh walking back to him. Both instances had touched Markham's heart.

Markham frowned. He crossed his feet on the lounge chair. Going sockless beneath the brown docksiders gave him a smooth tan.

Sluuuurrrrrrp!

Markham jumped and looked over.

"What's up, squirt?"

Sylvester lay on the lounge next to him and slurped the dregs of a daiquiri, a wedge of pineapple stuck to the rim. He wore the little paper umbrella that came with it behind his ear, and his bling-covered sand dollar hung around his neck.

"Sylvester!" said Markham.

"Squirt!" said Sylvester.

Markham shifted eagerly. "I haven't seen you since you helped me go after Nina."

Sylvester thrust himself a few inches farther away from Markham. "STOP BEING SO CLINGY!"

Markham actually laughed. "I got her. I found her. Thanks to you and Gavial." *And Crocidius.*

"Ohhhhh, you did?" said Sylvester, sounding disbelieving.

Markham's voice juddered, slightly offended. "I wouldn't be here if I didn't."

Sylvester took a long, rattling slurp from his straw. "It don't look like you got her." His voice was oddly wilted and serious.

Markham stared at him for a beat. And then his shoulders fell. He clicked the pen in his pocket once or twice to distract himself.

"No. It doesn't. She's shunning me."

"Good reason?" Sylvester gnawed on his straw and watched Markham with surprisingly innocent wide eyes.

Markham tensed up as he considered the question.

"No," he said tightly. "Not really."

Sylvester slurped again and continued to stare.

Markham glanced over his shoulder as a warm, salty breeze ruffled his silver hair and the collar of his palm-tree-embroidered manila Hawaiian shirt.

"Look, I . . . can you keep a secret?"

Slurp. Stare.

Markham leaned in close. He grasped the hot wood of the back of Sylvester's lounge chair. "We stumbled upon the Captain's cabin and found my signature in it. She thinks I'm the Captain."

Slurp. Stare.

Markham flicked up his eyebrows.

"Well?"

Sylvester released his straw and smacked his lips a few times, nodding.

"I could buy that," he finally said. Then nodded some more and looked at Markham. "Yep!"

"Please," Markham scoffed. He scratched at his sunburnt chest through the silky shirt.

"Well, you did pop in out of nowhere without remembering who you are, didn't ya?"

"I . . . yeah, but . . ." Markham struggled.

"Someone coulda thrown you overboard, don'tcha think?"

"Someone like Kloff? Yeah, his men could have thrown me overboard—as a random person he's framing. But as the real Captain?" countered Markham. "He saw me. He didn't recognize me."

"Sure about that?" Sylvester asked.

Markham thought. He remembered the way Kloff paused upon sight of him . . . how seconds later, he shot one of his henchmen.

The henchman responsible for the ridding of the Captain, maybe?

"Although maybe not with those scars on your face," said Sylvester.

Scars. *Is that why Crocidius mauled my face?* Cold blood stole through Markham. *Trying, and failing, to make me unrecognizable?*

"But your hair is silver and dignified!" Sylvester pointed.

"Thanks."

"Well shoot, squirt." Sylvester's voice hardened again as he squeezed the pineapple's juice into his empty glass. "If you really ain't the true Captain, you can at least try'n be Nina's, can'tcha?"

Markham froze. Sylvester was profound.

Gold light bled into tangerine sunset as shadows stretched like assassins behind them. A loud shout in some ancient-sounding language interrupted Markham's deep thought.

"Ooooh!" said Sylvester. "They're still doing it!" He stood and clapped his hands.

Markham sat forward.

Dancers and musicians in grass skirts and pink and orange leis filled the deck. Fire *whooshed* on twirling sticks, and pounding drums set their steps in rhythm. They struggled a little in the steep angle of the deck but carried the thick, carved tiki masks with expertise.

"Doing what?" said Markham.

"Singing to *you*, squirt!"

"Huh?"

The islanders began to sing a jubilant chant while raising and lowering their hands. Passengers packed into the deck and clapped along, more somber than Markham guessed they'd be under regular circumstances. Firelight reflected on faces streaming with tears. But their expressions were strong.

Sand dollar pendants—hundreds—rested confidently on their chests.

All of them.

"SALUTE THE TRUE CAPTAIN!" shouted the corpulent islander who began the procession. Abalone bracelets swirled teal and silver around his wrists, and angelfish paintings adorned his sand dollar. Everyone cheered, cursed Kloff, and saluted in the praising music.

Body after body passed around Markham as if he were a black rock amidst the motion of the ocean itself. He stood rooted, watching them go by in awe.

The parade leader shouted something in the island language again into the mob. Some understood and cheered. For the others, he translated.

"WE'LL SAIL SLANTED IF HE MAY REMAIN OUR TRUE CAPTAIN!"

Now everyone hailed.

The drumming intensified. The spinning sticks of fire were flung into the air. Markham looked around for Sylvester but found himself alone in the midst of it all.

The parade moved inside—cabin doors opened and banged closed as more joined them—and swept Markham with them. Fire dotted the darkness of all sixty balconies around the center opening. What seemed like the entire ship marched to the sixtieth floor like an army. They surrounded the Captain's uniform display, its glass reflecting hundreds of flames and faces.

Markham squeezed his eyes shut. So much more than beats pounded into him, but he couldn't place what. The deafening noise of voices and drums climaxed.

Then—silence.

Markham snapped his eyes open in shock.

Everyone was stiff as statues, saluting the Captain's jacket and hat.

His pulse quickened. He scanned all the brave and emotional faces.

And then something caught his eye. Something green.

One person was not looking at the display case.

Master Gavial stood tall, almost two feet above most of the passengers. Firelight boogied over his white jacket and emerald skin. His black eyes were alive, optimistic, and staring right at Markham.

Gavial didn't salute the case.

He saluted him.

Thwack!

A harpoon darted through the air above the crowd. Its rope tail zigzagged until it plunged into flesh.

"FOR KLOFF!" Kloffers raided the room screaming and hollering. The masses scrambled, but mobsters blocked the elevator, the only exit.

That island singer from before cried in pain and toppled over. The harpoon had speared him through the leg, and Kloff's minions now piled on top of him. Passengers tried to stop them but were punched and bitten and fell on their backs. The minions ejected more ropes into the air, which flew like snakes from cannons. Master Gavial fell to the ground writhing, tethered by endless cords.

The cronies raised the singer up above their heads as he moaned and reached for his bleeding leg. They twisted the parade into their own nightmarish procession with musically jarring, out-of-tune trumpets and marched the singer over to the balcony—the balcony that dropped sixty floors. Markham recognized one of the brutes—the enormous bowling ball one he'd met on his first day.

"WHERE YOUR CAPTAIN NOW?"

They dipped the lead singer over the edge of the rail, still holding on and looking around as if to see if anyone would answer before they let go.

Anger crashed into Markham's chest like a galleon colliding with an iceberg and splitting wood and mast. Suddenly he didn't want to just watch, didn't want to remain passive.

Didn't want to remain a mere passenger.

"Right here," he whispered, whether he believed it or not.

He bounded towards the gangsters.

"ANYWHERE?" the bowling ball goaded.

Closer. Markham bounded closer.

"NOOOOOOOO?"

They loosened their grip on the singer, who yelled.

Markham pulled the pen from his shirt pocket—the only weapon he had—and, out of nowhere, jumped up and grabbed the mobster's jaw, pulled it down, and shoved the pen down his throat.

Coughing. Hacking. Markham threw a punch into the other Kloffer as the first fell to his knees, cupping his throat, eyes wide and white with panic.

The last mobster holding the harpooned singer was losing his grasp. He glanced frantically at his two falling comrades and then at the dangling victim.

He decided not to hang around.

The mobster released the singer and ran off, and Markham dove for the rope of the harpoon.

He caught it and braced himself against the balcony. There was a jolt and a scream; Markham gripped the rope as the singer stopped falling, the harpoon barb keeping him suspended.

Though the man was twice his size, Markham slapped his hand farther down the rope. Again and again. Reeling him in. His palms were red.

Recovered passengers stepped forward to help Markham, and Kloffers pounded the back of the hot air balloon that was the choking mobster. Markham and a few others gathered the smooth-skinned grass skirt–wearing singer into their arms and fell backwards with him.

Cheers resounded.

Passengers swung fists or claws or tentacles and smacked the gangsters, herding them back.

Markham straightened, breathing hard. His chest jerked up and down. But the singer was safe.

He looked around at the miraculously spiked morale of the passengers and the Kloffers retreating to the elevator.

A crooked smile tugged at his lips. Pure understanding surged through him. Whether or not he really was the Captain . . .

He wanted to be.

The precision of that large, messy signature flashed in his mind. *I am the Captain—Markham Brody.*

Yes. He could envision himself signing it in microseconds while being tugged away, his bloody body overpowered by these minions . . . but fighting back. Fighting to return. Hoping his memory-washed self would soon find the page.

He didn't wait to watch the passengers turn the tide and run the gangsters back.

He sprinted into the elevator and slammed the down button.

As soon as the floor bobbed and the doors parted, he side-stepped through them and ran hard. Harder. Into a maze of red-carpeted hallways and hundreds of doors with porthole windows and brass room numbers.

When he reached the right room number, he banged on it.

Fire coursed through him. He jumped in place. Tossed his head. The moment felt like an eternity.

And then the lock turned, and the door opened tentatively.

Nina froze when she saw him, and then she scowled weakly. Her hair was a mess, her eyes bloodshot from either sleeplessness, seasickness, or crying.

"What are you doing here?" she asked.

"I'm here for *you,*" said Markham.

Nina scoffed. "You don't even know who you are, Markham." She started to close the door in his face.

Markham shot out a hand and stopped the door with startling force.

Nina actually jumped. A little of her old desire flickered in her gaze.

Markham leaned in. His voice was low and almost angry.

"*I'm your goddamn Captain.*"

Nina had time to grin before his hands reached her face and he dove inside the cabin.

NINETEEN

 said Markham.

Nina laughed. She hung from his arm and led him down the hall.

"We're going to *Gavial*, of course," said Nina.

"Is he ordained to marry people?" Markham flattened his hair with one hand.

Nina snorted. "I'm not marrying you." But then she tossed that shining look up at him again.

Suddenly the floor lurched up and wobbled, and Markham felt like he was crowd-surfing on top of it. They stumbled and fell against the slanted wall. Markham's palm pressed into the wall and his arm caged Nina in protectively. He sighed.

"This damn turn."

Nina sobered some, blinking and straightening off the wall.

She pulled his arm down and gently dragged him forward and up a metal staircase that led to the balcony awaiting the grand elevator.

As always, the great canyon of the ship's interior opened before them beyond the balcony. Murky figures glided along the levels of all floors. Only two stories below, the chandelier sparkled on wires. Its crystals hung at an angle like ice bullets falling sideways in a blizzard. Spots of white shone up at Markham and Nina, indicating set tables with spherical glass holders pulsing with candlelight. Some of Gavial's staff were crouched at the chairs, sliding bricks underneath the legs to level out the diners. Ropes crossed through the tables like graph paper, and the waiters used this to climb about the dining room and into the kitchen.

"So, Gavial because . . . ?" said Markham. "He's like a father to you?"

"Don't be offensive, Markham." He couldn't tell if she was kidding. "Gavial is like a science-lab pet to me."

"Is that better?"

Just as the iridescent panels of the giant elevator leveled into place, Markham looked down at Nina. Tears of love were in her eyes. He didn't question it.

They leaned on a wall as the elevator doors closed them in, and Markham planted his feet in front of him and crossed his arms. Other passengers chatted loudly, still dressed in ceremonial leaves and paint, too stoked up on drinks and fire to notice Markham in the back. Others hid in trench coats and enormous newspapers. One passenger was just a giant bumpy shell in the corner.

"Is someone in that?" Markham leaned over and whispered to Nina, eyebrows low. Dark grey sliminess stirred in the shell's depths, but it remained still.

"That was my fourth-grade teacher," she said. "Don't look at it."

"Your—?"

The elevator sprang open at the bottom floor, and the revelers hooted and raised their arms, surging in for dinner. Some of the waiters clapped and pulled out chairs. Silverware rolled down plates several times as the waiters caught it and reset it until it stayed still. Some servers shook their heads in frustration and walked off into the kitchen.

"*Come on,*" said Nina, tugging Markham past the dining area and into the galley.

Hisses, scrapes, and burbles surrounded their ears. Two of Gavial's young scampered over their feet and into the underside of the boilers.

"Gavial?" Nina called. She looked around. None of the station chefs paid her any mind, consulting menus and tapping their pocket watches. Finally Nina let go of Markham's arm and ambled forward.

"*Gavial?*"

Pop!

A bolt rained down over her head and bounced onto the floor. They looked up.

Crocidius' brown claw pried off the vent cover, and a moment later, the nostrils of his monstrous snout poked out. There was a growl.

"Crocidius!" Nina cried. "Markham—the most amazing thing—"

The growl spiked into a snarl. Markham could see saliva thread between Crocidius' long open jaw.

Nina faltered, pulling back in surprise. "He *saved* me. From *Kloff.* Doesn't that—"

Crocidius squirmed in the vent. They could hear his limbs slap the hollow metal, and he gurgled.

Nina huffed and shook her head. "Dammit, Crocidius! Just tell Gavial to come out and—"

Now two brown arms—one a stump—reached down and grabbed her by the shoulders. Her eyebrows shot up as he reeled her into the vent.

"Nina!" Markham jumped after her.

The same claw and arm gripped him a moment later and flung him into the vent as well.

He landed with a *smack* on cold, moist metal. It stank of mud and swamp. He looked up in time to see Crocidius' tail swish around the bend of the vent tunnel ahead.

Cursing, Markham crawled on his elbows after them. The metal pressed hard into his bones.

He reached a hole in the tunnel, and without even looking in, flopped down in a somersault and—

Sploosh!

—landed in cool, slimy water.

Bubbles belched to the surface, and he burst up. He gasped and looked around.

It was like a pet-store habitat in a metal box. An enormous bulb hung from the ceiling with no shade, reverberating heat off it like a sun. Sand encircled a large rock on which Master Gavial, for once undressed, lay. He was still in the way only a reptile could be, but it was more unnerving on his bright green skin and bead-black eyes. Markham always thought him the more human one.

Behind Gavial were framed photos: One of Nina as a toddler, sitting on top of Gavial's head with her tiny hands lovingly squeezing the bumps above his black eyes the way his young did. In the photo she was laughing as his eyeballs looked up at her. Another had a twelve-year-old Nina holding up a large cooked silver fish to Gavial in the kitchen. She wore a "Junior Sous Chef" jacket. Freckles that she had now outgrown splashed her face, and braces imprisoned her teeth. Gavial, in his white chef suit, beamed with an open jaw and held up his arms in praise.

Markham wondered where Nina had come from—why Gavial had to adopt her.

Over in the corner was Nina's bed. It was simple—a turquoise comforter. A firm pillow. Taped to the wall was her only piece of decoration: A poster of the underwater ocean. Vast, deep blue. It seemed to go on forever. Markham's eyes lingered on it for a beat.

Crocidius weaved smoothly like a snake through the small habitat and thumped onto the sand, leaving uneven tracks with his missing hand. Nina and Markham followed, and when Markham reached the shore, he actually shook like a dog and shivered. Gavial did not stir at their arrival. He looked nearly dead.

Crocidius rose to two feet and reared on Markham and Nina. His ghoulish eyes glared into Markham, and Markham swallowed what he hoped wasn't swamp water.

"What's gotten *into* you?" said Nina, sopping wet as well. Her expression was fierce despite her blue lips and the muck in her hair.

Crocidius paused for a long moment. And then he did yet another odd thing. He looked away, as if he couldn't answer her.

Nina tilted her head just slightly, and her expression softened. She touched his scaly arm.

"Crocidius?" Her voice was gentle.

He rumbled. She drew her hand away, folding it in her other, four-fingered one. Something between alarm and concern touched her eyes.

"Nina?" Markham took her shoulder in his hand and stepped forward. Nina hesitated, and then, slowly, she brushed his hand from her shoulder, keeping her eyes on Crocidius.

"We need to talk to Gavial." Her entire tone became impatient and robotic.

Crocidius did the closest thing to rolling his eyes and stepped aside. Markham passed him a curious glance before following Nina up the rock.

The surface was so hot that heat bled through the soles of his docksiders. He shifted weight back and forth to even out the cooking of his feet.

Nina crouched down and laid a loving hand over Gavial's green back.

"Master Gavial? Are you okay?"

He still didn't move.

"Nina, he's alive, right?" True fear sharpened Markham's voice.

"Yes," Nina replied instantly.

He sighed. But another shiver ran down his neck, and he saw Crocidius still staring at him, still bipedal, watching them from the small shore below the rock.

"Gavial, we have something to tell you, and we need you to help us. Crocidius was there; he saw the note. He knows I'm telling the truth."

Gavial stared forward blankly.

"Gavial, I know this is hard to believe, but . . . we've found the Captain." Her lips formed a hard line. She turned to Markham.

"Markham is the Captain."

Gavial gave a chirp. Nina actually jumped in shock.

"What?!" she said.

Gavial gave an identical chirp.

Nina's mouth dropped. "He says he knew."

"He what?" said Markham.

"Do you . . . are you saying you had a strong feeling?" said Nina. "Like you're not surprised?"

Gavial gave a chirp that even Markham could decipher as contradictory. Out of the corner of his eye, he could see Crocidius sneer.

"You knew *all along*?"

"Hold on a minute," Markham interjected. "You're telling me that you never thought I was a suspect, and you accused me for nothing?"

Gavial gave a growl that almost phonetically sounded like *Well* . . .

Markham crossed his arms. "Go on." He threw his head towards Nina. "Explain to her."

Gavial, at last, drew himself up. But this act seemed to take all of his heart.

Despite knowing he should be angry, something lifted in Markham's spirits, for animation trickled back into Gavial's movements, brightened his face, like a shower washing away dirt.

Gavial held out a claw in Crocidius' direction. Crocidius slumped over to the hat rack that held Gavial's chef hat and coat as well as Crocidius' black leather jacket. He reached down, took a board and marker from a chest of belongings next to the rack, and brought it to Gavial. Markham thought he caught a pile of crumpled-up documents with the Blue Star Line letterhead in the chest, too, but Crocidius had closed it fast.

The board was a whiteboard—a blackboard on the reverse. Gavial began writing on the whiteboard side. His hand was careful and neat.

Would he have found himself any other way? Certainly he wouldn't have taken my word for it.

He showed them the board. Markham recalled the room with the pillows, and his frown wavered. It was true that he hadn't exactly planned on ever leaving that room.

Gavial wrote on.

I have known Captain Brody for as long as this ship has floated.

"You mean…I'm not really twenty-six?" said Markham. "Why do I remember being twenty-six?"

The corner of Gavial's mouth seemed to twitch upward. He wrote,

Thousand. You're about twenty-six thousand.

Markham froze and whitened. Nina laughed with joy.

So, yes, wrote Gavial. *My, how long I've known you . . .*

He handed the board to Markham now. And then, with something like deep emotion in his eyes, the corners of his jaws pushed up as much as they could. He raised a claw to his forehead and saluted. Markham, holding the board in both hands, looked up at this great, benevolent beast saluting him once more. He could not speak.

Crocidius growled in disgust, something like *Get on with it.*

Gavial took the board back and continued writing.

I am one of only six on this ship who will recognize you by sight. Crocidius, Yastley, and the oldest gang lords all know who you are.

"That's why Kloff shot his henchman," Markham suddenly declared. He turned to Nina. "The second I walked into Kloff's chamber, Kloff shot someone. Probably the guy he trusted to get rid of me."

Gavial bowed his head as if to say, *Likely.*

"Why did they do this to him, Gavial?" said Nina.

Kloff is the youngest and stupidest mob lord on this ship. Obensteen is the oldest, and no one knows who he is, just like no one knows Captain Brody. Obensteen controls all of the casinos. He pays his men more, and Kloff is losing followers to him. They have been bitter rivals ever since . . .

He let them read, and then erased to write more.

Years ago, Kloff was a gangster for Obensteen, and he will do anything to usurp him. I suspect he devised a plan to put him at the top: Kill the Captain.

"*How* could he do that? When he's the—the stupidest . . ." Nina trailed off when she saw Gavial writing to answer her question.

He had help. Don't forget Babsy.

Markham glanced at Nina.

Babsy is the third mob lord, less talked about because he is a barnacle.

"He's also an idiot?" said Markham.

"No . . ." said Nina. "He's literally a barnacle. He lives under the ship, attached to it."

Our foulest prisoners are biogenetically altered to breathe water and sent to live with Babsy under the ship. But he has access to the deadliest assassins. Professionals.

Markham shuddered. "What does Babsy want with me?"

Probably to unleash all his prisoners onto the ship again.

"And Kloff plans to let that happen?" said Markham.

That is the least of what Kloff will do to this ship if he retains his current power.

"And why do you think they put the shirt on me? The Kloff one," said Markham.

I can only guess—but perhaps it was to signal to Babsy that the body floating by was really the Captain. Proof of a completed job.

"You mean they—" Markham began, but Nina groaned and interrupted.

"But he's *back,* Gavial!" Her voice broke with joy. "*Markham.* The Captain is back! He can put *everyone* down, restore things to as they should be!"

Not if no one believes he is the Captain.

"Why don't I have superpowers I can show off to them?" Markham said. "Mind control, levitation. This deal has got to come with something besides grey hair."

You indeed had powers . . . which have been taken from you, it seems. Even I do not understand the extent of these powers, or what falling overboard did to them. But you do not need superpowers to inspire your people.

"We'll show them the note Markham signed in his quarters," said Nina. "We'll testify."

Did that convince even the Captain Himself?

Nina looked at Markham. Markham looked at her and pursed his lips apologetically. His skin flushed pink with the heat from the lamp. Trouble crept through Nina's eyes, but she reached up with both hands to touch his silver stubble. It was a gesture saying, *How could they all not see what I do?* Markham closed his eyes, for he knew she would kiss him. She did, soft and slow.

Gavial watched like a wedding minister, pleased. But then he glanced uncomfortably at Crocidius and cleared his throat to break them apart.

"So, what should we do?" Markham spoke with strong, brave tones, then inhaled and wrapped his arm around Nina's shoulders.

Gavial's marker squeaked as he wrote.

Convince them.

"How?" Markham shot back.

The marker squeaked once more. It was losing ink.

Show the people that you will reverse whatever Kloff does. Start by re-lieving your people's pain, as you have always done: End the Great Turn.

Markham read this, and serious conviction hardened his face. It felt right. He thought deeply. Then he dragged his nails along his stubble and looked down. He froze.

Those little black frogs were sitting on his shoes and staring, wide-eyed, up at him. They must have appeared, as usual, when Markham and Nina were kissing.

Nina spotted them too. "HOW!" she squealed. Furious. Crocidius swiped one off his shoulder and hissed.

But suddenly, Markham huffed. "I know what I need to do."

Gavial couldn't help himself. He dropped his jaw in that large grin.

All of his teeth were stripped to the gums.

Before Nina could clap a hand to her mouth, Gavial's loving claw squeezed her shoulder. He shook his head reassuringly. Kloff's men must have knocked the crocodile's teeth out while detaining him.

Gavial wrote some more.

Go. Do what you must. Take Crocidius as protection.

Nina reached up to Gavial's snout, but Markham gathered her in his arms and nudged her towards the exit.

Markham stopped and looked up. "Gavial?"

Gavial wrote fast.

Yes . . . old friend?

"What was I like? Before this all happened?"

Gavial stared at him with something close to endearment for a long beat. And then he wrote.

You were grand.

TWENTY

Once out of the galley, Markham turned Nina to him.

"Nina, you know this ship better than anyone."

"That's not true," she said. He squeezed his hands on her and leaned down.

"It is. This ship is run by coal."

"Who said that?" said Nina.

"Me."

His gaze gripped her hard. There was something certain in it.

"All right . . ." she said tentatively.

"Where would the furnaces be kept?"

Nina laughed. "I don't know that, Markham! That's not a place any passenger could just . . . *go.*"

Markham frowned and looked around. Folks were scraping their chairs forward and grabbing the sides of the tables to stabilize themselves for dinner. None recognized him from the rally, and distress clenched his stomach. It would take something big to have them recognize him as their Captain once more.

"Come on." He marshalled Nina to the elevator with him, then whacked his fist below the up button and hit plain metal. "*Damn.*"

"This is the bottom floor," said Nina. "If the furnaces are in the belly of the ship, you're not getting to them by the elevator."

Markham rubbed his hand and nodded. "Any other ideas? Who might know?"

Nina placed both fists on his chest. "*Stop.* What is going on? What did those stupid little frogs make you think of?"

"Coal," said Markham. "They made me think of coal."

"And?"

"Stopping the Great Turn."

Nina thought for a moment, blinking.

"Wouldn't finding the anchor and dropping it be easier?"

Markham shook his head. "With our speed and the sharp turn, dropping anchor without slowing the propellers would capsize her."

How the hell did I know that? thought Markham.

Nina's lips had been fighting a smile as he spoke with such naval intelligence. "Yes, Captain . . ." She played with his ear. "I love when you talk nautical to me."

"Nautical can be our new dirty," he said with immediate intensity.

"It already is our new dirty."

They watched each other for a long beat. Then Markham cleared his throat.

"So," said Nina, "you want to get to the furnace to cut the—"

Markham covered her mouth with a hand. "*Shhh.*" He looked over her shoulder. "Anyone could be listening."

Nina nodded and pulled his hand down. "We need to talk somewhere safe."

"*How* is this safer?" said Markham.

Moss squished between his toes. His pant sleeves were scrunched up to his knees. The room was small and square with mirrors for walls and a thin layer of cool water on the ground. Farmers in conical palm-leaf hats dragged rakes over the mossy muck beneath the water. They reeled shiny black oysters to the surface in a slow, silent, methodical rhythm. The water rippled with soft rings like a Zen garden.

"Because it's a pearl farm and everyone here is really focused on what they're doing," said Nina, pretending to rake up oysters herself. Markham stood with his rake vertical in one hand.

"What?" he finally said.

"I just wanted to take you here," admitted Nina.

"That's what I thought." Markham sighed and went to work drawing his rake through the underwater soil.

"So . . ." Nina began, "the plan is to find the furnaces and shut them down. Even if we did find out *how* to get there, that sounds like something you need the Master Key for."

"What's that?"

"It's something only the First Mate carries. Can get into restricted parts of the ship."

"Then we need to talk to him!" Markham dropped his rake into the water, making a splash. None of the farmers looked up.

"He's being detained for insanity, Markham! No one will let you see him."

"I'm the Captain!" said Markham.

"Says us! And only us!"

"Then I need to *break* into where they're treating him. Breaking the rules on my own ship is always an option. Plus, who's detaining him?"

"Probably the infirmary," said Nina. "Security is very strict there."

"I bet Crocidius could help us crash that place. Gavial is right, we're going to need his help—even if only his brawn."

"Markham . . ."

"I know he plays both sides of the fence, too." Markham looked ahead and smacked his fist into his palm in a *eureka* gesture. "He's got ties with the mob lords that might be of use."

"Markham."

"I'm starting to trust him more."

"*Markham!*"

Markham swiveled in the water to look at her, alarmed.

Nina's entire expression was twisted with hurt. "Markham, Crocidius can't come. Or . . . we shouldn't be asking him to."

"Why?" said Markham. "What's wrong?" And then his face darkened. "He said something to you in their habitat, didn't he? I saw your expression."

"Nothing's wrong, it's just . . ."

Markham gave his head a slight turn and waited sternly.

"He's in love with me, Markham." Nina sighed and met his eyes. Markham's mouth dropped. "Crocidius is in love with me."

TWENTY-ONE

"That's the only reason he's been helping you." Nina tied her shoes back on as Markham returned his rake to a rack on the wall in the mudroom outside the pearl farm. He shook his head.

"I . . . don't understand."

"*What* don't you understand, Markham?" Fire reared in her voice. "He's *in love* with me. That's why he helped you rescue me. That's why it's hard for him to be around you."

"But—"

"But what?" said Nina. "He's a crocodile?"

Markham paused. "I mean . . ."

Nina shook her head and rose from the stool. Markham did a double take when he saw moisture in her eyes.

"Okay," said Markham, calming down and reaching to open the door for her. "What . . . like, he knew we were . . ." He shrugged. "That didn't stop him from helping us against Kloff before. What changed just now?"

Nina glanced up at Markham as if to say, *You forget quickly.*

Markham's eyebrows remained elevated as she stepped through the door and back into the seventh-floor halls. They passed upscale residential cabins with windowsill boxes of flamingo flowers on either side of the door.

Markham waited for Nina to go on, and she ruffled up as if annoyed that he still hadn't figured it out.

"He . . . smelled. That we . . ."

Markham pulled a quizzical expression when he thought he knew where she was going. Her voice had been tiny and sheepish for once.

"That's not awkward at all," Markham said at last.

"Well, you can imagine why that would upset him."

Silence lapsed, and in it, Markham truly felt a touch of sympathy for Crocidius. "I guess I'm not exactly his favorite person," he said at last.

"I'm not sure you ever were," said Nina, "even before this. This just sealed the deal."

"Was there something else I did to him that I don't know about?"

Nina rubbed her neck. "He applied to be First Mate, and you chose Yastley instead."

"I did?" said Markham. "I mean . . . oh."

Was that what all those Blue Star Line letters were in the chest? Rejections?

"He applied several times, actually . . . for almost a hundred years," said Nina.

"A hundred?"

"It was his dream to be First Mate," said Nina. "Yeah."

Markham thought about the black sand dollar amulet hanging

from Crocidius' neck, intentionally broken in half.

Nina went on to explain the partnership Crocidius and she had formed a few years prior, when Crocidius last attempted to win the Captain's favor. Her words painted the picture in Markham's mind.

Nina had jumped up onto double-stacked crates of flyers in a small room. She wore a button that featured Crocidius' long, intimidating snout, which had almost pushed up against the lens of the camera that had taken the photo, hiding the rest of his face. The flyer in her hand—and in the boxes, and on the walls—was one of several versions showing less-than-beautiful aquatic creatures. A blobfish on one. Goblin shark on another. A sea urchin looking like just a prickly pom pom of death. They reminded Markham of the creatures he'd seen in the slum on the way to Limbo to rescue Nina. Under each image were the words THE CAPTAIN'S PASSENGER or NOT FORGOTTEN. They implored readers to drop notes of support for Crocidius' application into the mailbox in the Captain's Parlor. Off to the side, Crocidius stood. He rested one sharp claw on a crate and looked at Nina. Shocking as the sight must have been . . . a genuine smile twisted around the crocodile's teeth and turned up at his cheeks. Crocidius . . . happy?

Markham turned a curious eye onto Nina again. "Have you . . . did you ever . . . *suspect* he had feelings for you?"

"He's hard to read," said Nina. "Looking back, some things make sense, but . . . no. Not at the time."

"I guess I understand leaving him alone now. But there are bigger problems in our future than love triangles. The passengers drove the Kloffers out yesterday for now, but they'll be back."

"I know," said Nina. "But I can't hurt Crocidius any more than I already have. We're just going to have to try to see the First Mate the normal way."

The beep of an IV threw off the ship's mood of tropical revelry. Everything in the lobby of the infirmary blared whiter than the flash of a camera—floors, walls, and furniture. Doctors consulting clipboards strode through the double doors by the front desk. A nurse leaned on a medical trolley like it was a shopping cart and pushed it into the operating room on the left. Hospital guards and security cameras were stationed at every corner.

"We'd like to visit Charleston Yastley please." Nina leaned on the front desk with Markham and watched as the secretary pecked keys at the computer. A parrot perched in a white cage behind her, its long red tail feathers penetrating the bottom of the cage.

"*WAWK! CHARLESTON YASTLEY.*"

"Loud bird," said Markham.

"One moment please . . ." The secretary pulled up the patient database and scrolled down. She didn't seem to recognize the name as the First Mate's.

Finally, she crossed her arms over the keyboard and looked up. "Charleston Yastley is not available for visitation at this time. I'm sorry."

"It's extremely important," said Nina. But Markham was already shaking his head.

"This was a bad idea."

"Ma'am, ever since the Great Turn, we've had *double* our normal intake of patients for nausea and vertigo. It's a busy building. And I hate to remind you that your friend Mr. Yastley is under surveillance for extreme erratic behavior and deemed dangerous to outsiders at this time." She peered at them through fake-diamond-studded horned-rimmed glasses. "I can give him a message when he wakes up from hypnotherapy tonight, though."

"So, they're dangling yo-yos in front of his face," sighed Nina.

But Markham darted over the counter and snatched a notepad. He wrote something down and folded it in half:

Yastley—I know who I am.
Markham Brody

"All right, fine. Give that to him. Let me know how he's doing after he reads it."

"WAWK! AFTER HE READS IT."

The secretary took the paper and slipped it into an envelope while the parrot dipped its black beak up and down.

Nina heaved a giant groan as Markham took her elbow. "Markham, we need to think of another plan." They turned around. "We're not getting the—"

They froze.

He stood there, on both feet, his neck stooped beneath the doorframe of the infirmary. His black jacket was around him, tattered and with a broken zipper, and his dinosaur-like tail curled on the floor in front of him.

"Crocidius," Nina whispered.

For the first time in Markham's entire life—that he remembered—he saw something soften in Crocidius' eyes. But the rest of Crocidius' manner remained guarded. His one claw and black nails were squished into fists.

The muscles in his great scaly neck bobbed up and down.

Nina listened, and then glanced at Markham. "He says we're wasting our time."

Markham rolled his eyes and cut forward. "Yeah, Crocidius. We know that."

A growl bowled from Crocidius' throat. Markham froze again and looked at him. Crocidius turned his long head and met Markham's gaze coldly.

Nina stepped between them. "That's not what he meant."

"Then what?" said Markham.

"He means we're wasting our time because Yastley no longer has the Master Key."

There was a long pause where all they heard was the awkward rhythm of IV drips and ringing phones. Markham stared up at Crocidius, whose vertical slit eyes rested just past him, but not on him.

"Are you going to help us?"

Crocidius pulled the whiteboard and marker from inside his jacket. He wrote.

I will lead you to the key. But not in service of the Captain.

Before Markham could respond, Nina cut in. "Thank you, Crocidius."

Crocidius inclined his head, away.

"How do you know who has the key?" said Markham.

Because I lost my claw trying to steal it back from them.

Shivers raced up Markham's spine. There was a pause of respect. The secretary, cowering behind her computer monitor, poked her head around it.

Kloff beat it from Yastley. And Obensteen's thugs beat it from Kloff's.

Suddenly it all came back to Markham. Kloff's gangsters booming into the sauna, confronting the mulberry-skinned pirates who were Obensteen's cronies, demanding to know where the "keys" were.

Markham nodded bravely. "Okay," he said. "Just take me to Obensteen. I'll do the rest."

You idiot.

Nina repulsed when she read this, how Crocidius would address the Captain, but Markham just allowed a twisted smile.

No one knows who Obensteen is, fool. Or do you forget the wisdom of my precious cousin so quickly?

"Then who would you lead us to?" said Markham.

Crocidius glared into Markham. And then he, too, seemed to give a twisted smile.

Are you feeling lucky?

TWENTY-TWO

Black and orange coal sizzled around them. The glowing char filled the entire area. In the middle of the room was a circular stage lit with black and purple lights to match the walls and ceiling. The temperature scorched Markham's skin, and the glow made his eyes water as he closed the door behind him. Slot machines the size of cars towered over drunk, happy gamblers lit in the neon lights. The machines flashed and rolled and spit dirty coins into plastic cups. Poker tables and mini golf courses dotted the casino like manicured shrubbery. Yellow tape closed off the mini golf, and a sign read:

Closed Until the Great Turn Ends

But that stage in the fire pit was the center of it all. It held only a table and two chairs. Brass piping rimmed its circumference.

A small creature with mulberry skin and a brass ring dangling from its prick ear sat in one of the chairs and was smoking wrapped-up seaweed that emitted brown fumes. Stacks of pink one-hundred-clam bills decorated with conch shells and seahorses tottered on his knees. The creature was grinning, looking around at all the patrons losing money and absorbing its toxins.

Crocidius rumbled behind Markham and Nina.

"He said that's the guy we want," said Nina. "He's the highest known crony of Obensteen . . . known as 'Mister Fortune.' He can't resist a gamble."

Markham drew in breath. He nodded. "All right." He cleared his throat. "And if this doesn't work out, you're going to go over there and—"

Crocidius gave that dark, burbling laugh. Markham knew how to interpret that one. *No. Good luck.*

Watching his feet carefully so as not to fall into the burning coal pit, Markham massaged his hands together and moved forward. He tried to make his voice strong and imposing. "HEY."

Mister Fortune set down his weed and squinted over at Nina and Markham from his little island in the middle of the coal sea.

"Get lost, sore losers." His voice was high and warty. He cackled and leaned back in his seat while fanning the wads of paper bills in his hands.

"I ain't here to lose, dumb-wad!"

"Ooh, nice," said Nina, only to Markham.

"Right?" Markham whispered back.

"I'd be furious," said Nina.

Mister Fortune ground his teeth at the insult. Markham yelled again across the popping embers.

"I'm here to win against Obensteen trash like *you*, coal-for-brain!"

Anger vibrated the side of Mister Fortune's mouth as he half rose from his seat, gripping the armrests. But after a moment . . .

"Pah!" Mister Fortune waved at Markham and went back to puffing.

"Snap," said Markham.

"No, no, I got you," said Nina.

"Okay, go for it."

"HEY!" Nina shouted this time. And when Mister Fortune looked over again, she lobbed a bright green golf ball at him. It smacked him square in the face and knocked him off his chair. His pink bills exploded in a halo of flaps.

"Oh!" Markham lifted a hand to his mouth. "Okay, damn!"

"Was that too much?" said Nina.

"How did you—I didn't even see you go over to the mini golf!" said Markham.

"I'm really fast," said Nina.

But now Mister Fortune recovered and stood up on top of his chair.

"You're gonna pay for that, Kloff piss!"

"Oh, yeah?!" shouted Nina.

"Okay, calm down," said Markham.

"Like hell!" cried Mister Fortune. "Get your sorry bums over here if you're not gonna run to mommy first!"

"Oh, boy," said Markham. He looked around the rim of the coal basin for a set of stairs or a path for safe crossing. There were none.

"This is what we came for," said Nina. "Come on."

Markham nodded. He braced his muscles, gave a quick, pointed glance at Nina . . .

Then swung down into orange coals.

Heat swallowed him. His body coiled in fear, and beneath his shoes, coal broke and dissolved, then cracked louder. He balanced himself and darted his eyes around at all the sparks rising to make the air blurry. He gulped.

Mister Fortune watched with great interest and gave a toothy smile.

Nina groaned behind Markham and jumped down too. "*Ow!* Hot!" She gave him a shove in the back. "*Move,* Captain Clueless." They winced and crunched their way fast to the island in the center.

Markham jumped and grabbed hold of the brass rail, then hauled himself up, cursing at the heat of the metal. He turned and lifted Nina into his arms with both hands.

"Impressive, for a Kloffer." Mister Fortune sneered. His pupils were sevens like from a slot machine, dilated from the weed. "Now give me *one* reason why I shouldn't spin your head around like a roulette wheel."

"Because I'm no Kloffer," said Markham, and he boldly took a seat across from Mister Fortune. "I'm the *Captain.*" Everyone in earshot hooted mockingly, hitting each other with jest as if to say, *Get a load of this clown.* "And I want to challenge you to a gamble."

Mister Fortune laughed—a sound like steam screeching from a teapot. He crept forward on the table. "And what would that be?"

"I know you have the Master Key."

Mister Fortune froze. He narrowed his slot machine eyes. "How?"

"Never mind that," said Nina behind Markham. Mister Fortune snapped his attention up at her and bared his teeth.

"What would you propose?"

"I play you at the game of your choice," said Markham. "If I win, you give me the Key. We make it a public spectacle, so that you're bound to give me my dues if you want to uphold the reputation of your casino."

"And if I win?"

Markham leaned back as if he wasn't worried at all. "What do you want?"

But Markham regretted it the second he spoke, for he realized Mister Fortune's eyes were already fixed on Nina. He rubbed the welt forming on his face where Nina's golf ball had hit him.

"Pretty girl you've got there . . ."

Markham opened his mouth to object.

"*Deal*," said Nina. Markham jerked around to look at her.

The crowd gathering around the island all said, "Oooo . . ."

Mister Fortune snickered again and scraped his chair forward at the table.

Markham mouthed, *Nina!*

She rolled her eyes. "Play."

Mister Fortune piped up loud enough for the whole casino to hear over the jingles and rattles.

"GET ME A DEALER!"

In a matter of minutes, a bow-tied dealer with merman features— webbed fingers and elbows—joined their table. Crowds of spectators rimmed the basin of hot coals, dangling their feet but not touching the char. They made bets and tossed popcorn into their mouths.

"All right, toots." Mister Fortune produced two tankards from underneath the table that were covered in buckles and studs like treasure chests and placed them on the surface. "Here's the game." Mister Fortune gestured at the dealer with his head and waited with his hands crossed on the table.

The dealer took the tankards and turned to the brass railing. Markham leaned over and peered at what he was doing.

A faucet dipped down from one of the rails that he hadn't before seen. The dealer twisted a knob and liquid streamed into the mugs.

He set one each before Markham and Mister Fortune.

Mister Fortune raised his tankard. "You asked for the game of my choice. Well, here it is."

Markham lifted his mug and gazed into the frothy water. It smelled of salt. "You're not serious."

"Delirium Drinking," said Mister Fortune. "This stage is our life raft. The coal around us? The ocean. We drink as many rounds as it takes for the first man to succumb to insanity and fall off the stage. The one still on board wins." He turned and raised his tankard to the audience, who cheered madly. His smile was devilish. "Ready, pops?"

Markham ran a hand through his grey hair and sighed.

They lifted the tankards to their lips as the crowd battered their fists in unison on the floor in anticipation. Markham squeezed his eyes closed hard and gulped.

The salt slipped too easily into his throat and tingled down his chest.

They banged their tankards down.

Foam lined Mister Fortune's upper lip and he wiped it away with the back of his hand. He dropped his mouth and laughed while the dealer refilled their mugs.

Now the foam surged over the rim and trickled onto Markham's hand. His stomach churned at the sight of it.

"TWO!" the dealer boomed.

Markham and Mister Fortune threw back the drinks like shots, downing them in four large gulps.

Markham gasped for breath and knocked the tankard onto the table. The saltwater left fire in his throat, but unlike alcohol, it suffocated and twisted his stomach all at once.

Mister Fortune was grumbling and wincing, but he thrust his mug towards the dealer for the next round.

"THREE!" shouted the dealer. Markham could hear Nina fidget behind him, but his fingers scrambled to collect the filled tankard.

"Getting—*hic*—loopy, silver fox?" said Mister Fortune, reeling his own mug into him.

"Not—*hic*—a chance."

They downed the drinks. More than a quarter of Markham's spilled over his face and onto his shirt, but the dealer didn't call it, for Mister Fortune did the same.

This time when Markham dropped the tankard, it skipped off the table and the dealer caught it with one hand.

"FOUR!"

The dealer set each tankard down at the same time in front of the drinkers, one in either hand.

Desperate thirst dragged nails down Markham's throat. But the sight of the bubbling, seething water nearly made him vomit. Mister Fortune didn't speak either as he wobbled the mug up to his face.

They pumped in the water.

This time instead of dumping into him, the saltwater rushed up to his head and swirled it like a whirlpool. He could almost hear the swish and gurgle and bubbles streaming up from his lips. Images flashed back to him. Pictures.

Markham Brody. Lights flashed on a billboard again.

He felt all his power—godlike power—clap out of him as his

body hit the surface of the open ocean with the sound of cosmic thunder.

The talons of a seagull ripped at his nose.

Now Markham's face twisted. He dropped his jaw and let this tongue feel the air on its salty buds.

"FIVE!"

He stood on the marble floors of the sixtieth level. Those towering windows poured in sunlight. No one was with him except for the tall green figure of Master Gavial. Markham stepped up to a mannequin that was already wearing the dark blue, gold-studded Captain's coat. He lifted his hands to his head and pulled off the Captain's white hat. Placed it over the mannequin.

Are you sure, Captain? He'd understood Gavial's chirps perfectly and smiled.

"They need it more than I."

Gavial, endeared, smiled back. Markham placed a hand on his shoulder.

"SIX!"

The table morphed into a desk. A blueprint of the ship and a large, gridded antique map sprawled over it. Weights kept the corners from curling back in. He scrawled tiny print in the margins of the documents and looked up.

Little frogs lined his desk. Their inky feet splotched dark spots over a sealed missive. Markham chuckled and took the envelope. He sliced it open.

"Furnace report?"

They stared at him blankly.

"And . . . nope. Breeding report. Of course. Twenty thousand more offspring last month."

Continued blank stares.

"Horny little tree-lickers." He shooed them off with the back of his hand.

"SEVEN!"

Markham clutched his stomach after gulping then retched forward. He looked up, dazed, and saw First Mate Yastley standing at the doorway to his cabin. Yastley's expression mixed sadness and affection. He wore his white naval jacket with silver buttons and epaulettes.

"Sir, do you recall last week's message to the passengers?"

Markham felt heavier, crisper clothes on his body. This must have been longer ago than the images at the mannequin. He pursed his lips. His voice was gentle yet powerful. "I couldn't forget that one, Yastley."

Yastley nodded and left Markham's sight for a moment. When he returned, he was gazing down at a human infant wrapped in bundles of fleece in his arms. He walked up to Markham, and Markham pushed out his chair, resting a strong hand on his desktop. He frowned.

"My latest decree to my people." Yastley recited Markham's words from the week prior while keeping soft eyes on the face of the baby. His voice was a whisper. "If anyone's infant shall be near death, they may bring them to rest in my arms if they so wish." Yastley looked up at Markham. "She is sick, sir. She is near to departing from your deck."

Markham opened his arms. Yastley leaned down and carefully slipped the child into Markham's grasp.

Markham coiled his arms tighter around the infant and laid her over his chest. "Leave us," he whispered. He leaned back and closed his eyes, clutching the weak, sleeping baby to him, one large hand over the back of her tiny head.

Yastley watched with tears dripping down his cheeks. He nodded. Again and again.

"EIGHT!"

Now the memories looked like brushstrokes in a painting. Markham swiped a punch. A trident glinted. It tore his shirt.

More tridents. Death ahead.

He stumbled backwards onto a balcony above the ocean.

Looked down.

Placed a hand on the bulwark . . .

Something sizzled loud, like a fresh hamburger patty being pressed into the grill.

"WINNER!" the dealer shouted. The audience erupted.

"Markham!" Nina shook him. "Markham, you won!"

"Wha—?" Markham slurred off, and then he rubbed Nina's arm. "This . . . nice. This is nice."

"My arm?" said Nina.

"Yeah. This is nice."

"GET ME A FIRE EXTINGUISHER!" shouted the dealer, and some of Obensteen's fellow cronies loped over to help Mister Fortune rinse off the burning coal. He howled in pain as they carried him away, and others laid a bridge over the coal for them to climb onto.

"And you," said the dealer, turning to Nina. "Just get that boy to a urinal. That poison needs to leave his body pronto."

Markham stood and hobbled off with Nina across the bridge.

"Or . . . a dark corner," said Markham.

"Yep," said Nina. She tugged him past a few rows of slot machines and card tables as people clapped for them. Everything became sparser. "Here." Nina pushed him into just that—a dark corner in the casino. "Just go. I'm going to go demand that key before they forget . . ."

Markham fell against the wall and groaned. "This . . . this wall is nice."

"Yes, it's very nice."

He started relieving himself. The carpet darkened at his feet.

Nina scanned the crowd for the dealer. Her eyes narrowed. "Where is that son of a—"

"Very beautiful woman, I hope you were going to say." The tall bow-tied dealer strolled up and presented what was clearly a large brass key capsuled in bubble-wrap. "No unfair gambles on my table, miss."

Nina accepted the Key in both hands and laughed. "Markham you *did* it!"

"Huh? That's nice," said Markham from the wall.

The dealer looked over Nina's shoulder at Markham still thudding urine onto the carpet. Nina twisted, following his gaze.

"Yeah . . . about that . . ."

The dealer grunted dismissively. "No one has *ever* beaten Mister Fortune at a game. The players will be hearing about this."

He looked at Nina with a thoughtful gaze and paused. "Maybe he is the Captain."

TWENTY-THREE

Markham awoke to bangs outside his cabin door. Up and down halls he heard fists batter on doors and handles jingle and voices shout.

He rubbed his eye and sat up. Dryness cracked his lips, and a headache sawed at his temple.

Something heavy slid down the covers when he shifted, and he turned to the eight-inch-long brass skeleton key, which was engraved with the Blue Star Line emblem and the words MASTER KEY on its stem. Its patina was aged and blotchy, and when he lifted it, it felt like almost two pounds. He held its cold metal in both hands.

The banging and shouting continued, seeming to match his headache and dehydration pangs as he wobbled over to the dresser where a note lay.

Markham—I had to find Crocidius and talk to him. Here's the key. I'll meet up with you as soon as you wake.
- N

"OPEN, DAMMIT!" someone yelled. Markham couldn't take it. He shook his head and stormed out of his cabin with the Master Key clutched in his fist.

"WHAT the HELL is going o—?!"

"DON'T CLOSE YOUR DOOR!" a woman—his neighbor, with an apricot veil around her head—yelled, but Markham's cabin door had already swung closed and clicked shut. He turned to it, dumbfounded.

Others were tugging and knocking at their cabin doors, locked out. Markham, mouth open, dug out his keycard and swiped it into the cabin lock.

The light flashed red. He swiped again.

Red.

Red.

He tried the Master Key when no one was looking, but the slot was only for keycards. The First Mate didn't have access to personal quarters, then.

"My baby!" someone cried down the hall. "My baby's inside!"

"WHAT IS GOING ON?!" Markham shouted.

"None of our cards are working," said the woman with the apricot veil. "We're locked out."

"Who did this?!" The distraught mother down the hall sobbed. "My baby . . ."

Markham's brow lowered. He moved out of the hall, weaving around angry, worried figures standing outside of their homes.

Out on the balconies, more mayhem echoed on the other floors. He could make out silhouettes shaking fists and rushing for the elevator . . .

"*Ooph!*"

Markham bumped into a wall of bodies. A thick crowd of loud bickering passengers accumulated at the elevator stop, all clutching keycards, all, no doubt, heading for the Mess to find that bullet-infested door into Kloff's territory and the keycard reception desk run by teenagers.

As soon as the elevator opened, people swarmed in, yammering as loudly as ever. Markham dove forward and rammed himself through the edges just in time. Bodies pressed him against the wall.

They yattered on like a flock of birds as the elevator swooped down and opened—sure enough—to the Mess. The lettered arch crowned the opening into that enormous city-like world, but those from the elevator marched on fearlessly, some waving keycards in the air and some grabbing sticks from the street. Markham could finally pick out words.

"KLOFF!"

"KLOFF'S A MENACE, HE IS!"

"THE CHECK-IN OFFICE! LET'S GET HIM!"

As Markham stayed behind, the elevator doors dinged open again and let out another mob of angry passengers, flowing right in the same direction. They sucked him into their current, and he paraded along, down the brown-and-grey streets of the Mess. Between bodies Markham caught a glimpse of that violinist he'd seen playing here so long ago. They were still obscured in that boxy trench coat, grasping a violin by the neck and hanging it at their side. The violist leaned back on the wall and watched as the passengers trooped on. Markham thought he saw the swish of a tabby tail between their feet.

Soon, shoes stomped up the brightly lit stairs and that revolving door spun like a top. Markham tripped into the revolving door and was flung around, then staggered forward into the hotel lobby.

Then, to his alarm, despite the massive crowd of people . . .

Silence.

He edged forward.

A berth encircled the bullet-riddled door to the crude check-in office. And before it stood those two bullish gunners, grey muscles bulging like boulders in a catapult, bursting past ripped clothes. They gripped those huge machine guns low at their fronts, and their eyes were veiny and red. The passengers grew whiter as they looked down the *many* barrels of the machine guns.

"You want room . . . YOU SALUTE *KLOFF!*" boomed one of the bulls, so loud that those at the front fell back trembling and had to be caught by their peers. "You don't salute Kloff, we send you underwater to BABSY!"

"If you have problem with those options . . ."

The second bull squeezed the trigger. The gun's barrels slowly started to rotate, and passengers screamed in horror, running for the door. At the last moment, the bull pulled the gun up to the ceiling and battered the roof with bullets. Markham turned away and covered his head with his arm as drywall showered down.

By the time most passengers had cleared out, the bulls rumbled with laughter, and smoke furled from the machine gun.

"Stinkin' right ol' bulls needta be broke is what they need, mmm-hmm, yessir."

Markham knew that voice. The bulls turned to it in curiosity, looking past the open doorway into some abandoned hotel rooms. They saw the elegant curve of a cowboy boot tapping the floor, the rest of the figure sitting in the chair out of sight.

"*Markham!*" a voice hissed.

Markham spun around. Nina was crouching behind one of the golden trollies, hand holding the rail. She rose only a few inches, then hissed at him some more.

"*Come here!*"

Markham ducked over as the rest of the passengers fled, the bulls standing their ground.

"Kloff disabled all the keycards," said Nina.

"I know," said Markham. "One woman's baby is locked inside on my floor."

"And the passengers will kill each other without their space." Nina looked around, serious distress on her face.

"We need to get moving," said Markham.

"Please tell me you took the Master Key out of your room." Nina stared at him wide-eyed.

He glanced over his shoulder once and produced the large key from his pocket just halfway, so she could see.

"Thank the Captain," she breathed.

Markham twitched a half smile. "You're welcome. Let's go." He prodded her through the revolving door and back into the Mess' streets, which were quickly emptying as people scrambled to spread the news the bulls had delivered.

Nina and Markham took a few steps down the street towards the elevator when Markham shoved her into a dark alley.

"Markham?!"

He stepped with her to the cold, dank wall. "Kiss me."

Nina moaned. "This isn't the time, Markham!"

"Dammit, just kiss me!"

"Stop being a pervert!"

Markham groaned and slammed his mouth to hers. He didn't intend to make much out of it, but he tasted her and moved against her, and it was like another shot of seawater to his head.

He pulled back. She breathed hard.

"Damn . . ." he whispered, looking around.

"What, that wasn't good enough for you?" said Nina.

"*Shhh . . .*" He laid a hand over her mouth, still looking around. "I just forgot they were black."

"*What are you*—UGH!"

Markham turned to follow Nina's gaze. Yellow eyes stared at them from the lid of a shadowed dumpster.

"CATCH ONE!" said Markham. He pelted for the little frogs and banged into the dumpster lid. They flopped onto the dirty ground and slapped off in opposite directions. "CATCH ONE!"

Nina swept a hand down to intercept one of the tiny frogs mi-djump but missed by so little that black ink scraped onto her hand.

Markham dove into a street puddle of brown and silver that swirled with sparkly oil. He clapped his hands together in front of him.

Nina crouched down next to him and bent her head close to his closed fist—the rest of the frogs were already out of sight.

"Open just a crack," she said. "I'll tell you if it's in there."

He obeyed.

Nina shook her head and rose, and Markham nearly gave a cry of despair.

Then Nina smiled deviously.

"Horny little tree-licker," said Markham. He grinned broadly until he realized how close his mouth was to the foul street water. "I get it?"

"Yeah." Nina nodded. "You got it."

TWENTY-FOUR

"Awwwmigosh. Okay. We're never yelling at them again. Look at it." Nina leaned down and inspected the little black frog.

It lifted its bulging yellow eyes from where it was squished under Markham's thumb. Its face was sad, expressive, and disgustingly adorable.

"We need to make a little leash for it," said Markham, taking careful steps lest the frog bolt from his closed fist. They passed beneath the signpost arch and neared the queue for the elevator. "It's going to show us where the boiler room is."

Nina scrunched her face together. "That's the randomest thing I've ever heard."

"Are you serious?" Markham pinned her with an *are-you-serious?* look to accompany the question. It was a pretty random ship.

"Why would it have any idea?" said Nina.

Markham paused. Should he tell her of the visions he'd seen while drunk on seawater? Did he have reasonable evidence to trust those . . .

Memories?

"Look, it's hard to ex—"

Something smacked him on the side of the face.

"Markham!"

He stumbled aside and squeezed his fist harder over the little frog so it wouldn't escape. Except . . .

Whatever struck him didn't fall. It inhaled his skin and sucked it in . . . and in . . . and . . .

Markham screamed in pain and tried to claw the thing off. It felt rubbery and slick. And as he mauled it more, he realized . . .

It pulsed. It was alive.

"Hold still!" Nina gripped it with both hands and pulled. It popped off with the sound of hundreds of suction cups bursting loose.

"What's going on?!" Markham shouted. Red welts already formed on the side of his face.

THHHWOOP!

Another squid splat onto Nina's arm and clasped on like a grappling hook.

"RUN!" said Nina, tearing it off before it sucked too deep.

They bolted for the elevator, and Markham looked over his shoulder.

Three figures ran after them holding bazooka-looking guns, the barrels opening wide at the end like blunderbusses. The figures had finned joints and webbed fingers. Some kind of bowl covered their faces, and dirty seaweed swirled in the water that filled it.

"WHO THE HELL ARE THEY?" yelled Markham.

Nina sprinted alongside him. "MY EX-BOYFRIENDS!"

Markham shot her an aghast look and Nina, panting, yelled, "HOW AM I SUPPOSED TO KNOW WHO'S TRYING TO KILL US, MARKHAM?"

Another squid flew past them, and Markham ducked. The squid hit the ground and tumbled over its tentacles. Nina leapt over it and started shoving people aside at the queue for the elevator. Luckily chaos was already pretty high—all were too busy hollering, waving their keycards, and shoving people themselves to notice anything. Nina pushed herself to the rail of the balcony and craned up her neck.

"Dammit!" said Nina. The elevator was at least twenty stories up and moving slowly. Markham gasped, clawing his chest, and came up beside her. He hung onto the rail too, keeping his eyes over his shoulder.

"Gotta do something, Nina," he said, seeing the strange maritime assassins gain ground between the crowd. "Gotta—"

A squid hit his leg, and he buckled over. It squeezed ferociously, throbbing with hunger, and Markham screamed again. Blood burst in his foot like the juices of a stress ball ballooning to one side when squeezed.

Once the other passengers noticed the assassins, they squealed and backed into the walls or fled back through the archway of the Mess.

"GOTTA DO SOMETHINGGGG!" Markham groaned.

"We're gonna jump, Markham," said Nina.

Markham's face was glowing; he rattled in breath. The assassins loaded another squid and raised their guns right to their own faces.

Nina grabbed Markham's shirt by the fistful. "JUMP!"

She hauled him over the rail, and they plummeted.

Air slipped over them. The fall was smooth and fast. Nina reached out, and, with one hand still tethering Markham to her, snatched hold of the wire of the chandelier over the dining room. Markham swung out a hand and did the same, and they thudded down the wire like firemen on a pole until—

Crash!

They hit the chandelier, and it rocked to the side, tinkling thousands of crystal teardrops. The lights flickered, and those in the dining room gave a collective "Oh!" and looked up. Several beings scraped back their seats and stood.

Nina tried to share a look with Markham, but Markham's eyes were rolling with pain. The squid had gnawed into his skin deep enough now that blood streamed down his leg.

She shouted for help.

Muscles pulsed in Gavial's neck, and his eyes flared. He made angry gulping noises at Crocidius, who turned his long brown snout away and stared fire into the ceiling. Gavial motioned a claw towards Markham and crackled more. Crocidius snarled and shoved Gavial's arm down.

"It's not his fault, Gavial," said Nina in a little voice, near Markham. Markham lay on two dinner tables pushed together. His eyes were closed tightly, but he refused to moan in pain as Nina cleaned the wound the squid had inflicted. His foot was still blue from blood clotting. "Crocidius didn't know we'd be pursued."

Gavial instantly chirped a response.

"He's not our bodyguard," said Nina. She lifted Markham's leg and placed gauze beneath it, starting to wrap the wound. "We don't even know why—" She stopped.

Markham, alarmed, lifted his head, one brow raised.

"Gavial," said Nina.

Gavial stalked over with a grim face. He slowly latched his claws together behind his back.

"Look." Nina indicated the scar left by the squid. Now Markham clambered to sit up and see for himself.

Within every circular suction cup scar, a *B* could be seen.

Gavial gave a long, dark hum. Nina looked at him, and he grunted at the same time she said, "Babsy."

"Babsy?" said Markham, a little breathless. For some reason, he glanced at Crocidius. His heart lurched. The tips of Crocidius' jaws seemed to be . . . lifted.

Nina nodded. "Remember we mentioned Babsy's connection with professional assassins."

"Right," said Markham, forcing himself to look away from Crocidius. But his head spun with conspiracy.

"And these assassins were wearing water helmets—which makes sense, since Babsy's men are from the prisons on the outside hull of the ship," said Nina.

"Okay," said Markham.

"And now Kloff knows his gangsters failed to kill you." Nina finished tying the gauze and placed both of her hands over his leg, not looking at him. "He must have told Babsy to finish the job." She leaned down, kissed the bandage, and then looked at Markham. "They won't stop."

Markham nodded and swallowed. "I know."

Gavial laid a hand on Nina's shoulder and grumbled something. Nina nodded.

"We need people other than the enemy to begin understanding who you are," Nina translated.

Markham hummed a short note of acknowledgment—and dread. Before he opened his mouth, he sighed, as if regretting what he was about to say. "I have an idea."

"You do?" said Nina.

Another labored breath. "Unfortunately."

"Is it that bad?"

"Yes," said Markham.

"What does it involve?"

"Sylvester."

"Oh . . ." Nina's tone clearly shared his dismay, and Gavial groaned in mutual understanding behind her. "Okay," she said. "We'll . . . come back to that. But way more important first—do you still have the frog?"

Markham dug his hand into his pocket, then spread open his palm. The frog was there, shaking, but unscathed.

Nina took it delicately in her hands. "I'll go in the kitchen and find something to tie a leash with."

She left for the galley. Gavial stood there with his great reptilian head hung in thought. He exuded that scent of jasmine and mystery, but his claws were still curled into stressed, angry fists behind his back. He turned towards Crocidius and crept slowly after Nina, still bipedal but with his tail slithering in his wake. As the two crocodiles passed one another, they turned their heads to lock black eyes—Crocidius' like blades and Gavial's like marbles. Silent tension shivered between them. Gavial pushed open the galley door and disappeared inside.

Markham's heart pounded. He watched Crocidius, who stood rock still.

Then the nightmarish brown head turned to Markham. Crocidius' teeth oozed with drool that snaked out of his mouth in all different directions. He moved to Markham.

At his side, Crocidius towered over Markham and glared down at him.

"You meant to leave us at the casino," Markham whispered. Crocidius did not move. "You knew they were coming."

Markham's heart was pounding. For a long time, Crocidius did not move.

"Killing me won't make you First Mate," said Markham, in an attempt to be bold—an attempt to hit Crocidius in where Markham thought was his core. But Markham's voice was hollow. "What makes you think you can do this job better than the others?" said Markham. "I rejected your applications for a hundred years. I'd think I'd had a reason."

Crocidius, having no dry-erase board and no way to talk to Markham, slinked around the makeshift stretcher and over to the wall. Using his long nail, he scraped something into the drywall. Markham shifted to see, but he shook with nerves.

When Crocidius stepped aside, Markham read his graffitied sentence.

THEY ARE ALL YOUR PASSENGERS.

Crocidius stared at him pointedly.

Markham swallowed. He remembered those flyers Nina described, the ones with the most twisted species of the ocean. "Babsy, Kloff . . ." said Markham.

Crocidius nodded.

It started to make sense. Crocidius dealt with, formed bonds with, the gangsters, the unsightly. It never occurred to Markham that maybe, somewhere down the line, his own neglect had caused the mob lords' resentment. Perhaps no First Mate he'd chosen had ever connected with *all* of his passengers, even the slimiest and strangest.

"That's what you want," said Markham. "To represent them all."

Crocidius' stillness seemed to confirm it. And Markham could see it now—could see Crocidius as the emblem of acceptance and unity for the gloomy populations of the ship. The opposite of the clean white coat Yastley and other First Mates had worn for centuries.

"Then why didn't you let them kill me before?" said Markham. "And take over the ship without me?" But then it dawned on him. Crocidius had in fact helped him all along—biting his leg to keep him from entering Kloff's territory where he could be recognized, trying to disguise his face from Kloff, saving him from the prison cell, leading him back to the main decks from the Captain's Quarters . . .

Crocidius only really wanted him dead after Markham and Nina . . .

"She chose me," said Markham at last. This time his voice was completely sure. "That's it. *That's* when you wanted me dead."

Crocidius continued to stare at Markham. Then he approached, reeking of swamp and something else, something that made Markham's breath catch with fear.

He brushed a long, sharp claw along the welt on the side of Markham's face and turned away.

TWENTY-FIVE

Wires ran stapled along the floor. Pressboard walls closed off black umbrella-like stands and ultraviolet light fixtures. The room was cool and dark.

Markham and Nina had made it to the thirty-fourth deck. They'd passed fuzzy red stanchions marking the entrance to a theater lit up in exposed bulbs, tall black letters alight over the ticket booth. A poster for a movie called *Carpathia* was in a glass shadowbox next to the entrance. It featured the bow of a ship and two lovers translucent in the sky above it. Just past there was the door marked SILLY STUDIO.

The sound of a steady rotating lever had clicked through it.

Nina held Markham's arm as he limped forward as quietly as possible. Once again, though, Dr. Flabberstein's ointment was working its magic.

"Are you okay?" she whispered, glancing over at him. "You look . . . troubled. I mean, more than usual."

Markham shivered. Crocidius' claw seemed to brush down his skin again. Were those fiery black eyes gazing into his hoping to watch him die, or live?

"It's nothing," Markham said.

It was past midnight. The studio entrance had led them through the wide, spooky theater with escalating rows of empty red seats and a blank grey screen at the wall. The EXIT sign had still been alight, and once they'd stepped through, pursuing the clicking sound . . .

"That's the stuff," said Sylvester, somewhere in the maze of board walls. The lever continued to click. "Oooh, that's hot . . ."

Markham froze. He shared a mutually horrified look with Nina. "No," Markham whispered.

"Oh god . . ." said Nina.

They followed the clicking noise, finally stepping over a large coil of wires and around the bend of a wall to see what all those tall neon light fixtures flooded down on. Almost everything—the walls and floors—was still black, but in the middle . . .

A silver table stood beneath the spotlights and fill lights. Across the table, Sylvester stood on a stool, one eye dipped into the lens of a long purple camera. He slowly rolled the lever on the side of the camera, feeding 35 mm film through it. Clappers and a director's horn were behind him.

"Ooooh, mama!" he said.

Markham followed the gaze of the camera to the table again. This time he noticed two frozen shrimp lying flat on the table and baking in the light.

"Is this adult entertainment or a cooking show?" Nina whispered.

"VIEWER DISCRETION IS *ADVISED!*" Sylvester cried triumphantly. He still didn't see their arrival.

Markham sighed and covered his face.

"Oh, Markham . . ." said Nina. She visored the side of her eyes with a hand.

"Sylvester?" Markham spoke from his still-covered face.

Sylvester yelped and sprang from the camera. He saw them, and the antenna sticking out of his sleeve zapped with static. "Squirt!"

"Hey . . ." Markham let his hand fall. He took a step closer. "So, yeah. What's . . . What's going on here?"

Sylvester gave a naughty chuckle.

"Please tell me those are just two pieces of shrimp," said Markham.

"Prawn stars," Sylvester corrected.

Markham and Nina gave huge nods, then looked at each other. *Of course.*

Sylvester glanced back at the table, googly-eyed with admiration.

"We need a favor." Markham didn't waste any time.

"Striking!" said Sylvester. He flicked on the overhead lights, and Markham and Nina winced. "Anything, squirt."

"I'm the Captain," said Markham.

Sylvester rubbed his hands together and nodded as if he knew this all along.

"We need other people to believe it, though, if we're going to stop Kloff," said Markham. "I'm about to go into the furnace and stop the Great Turn. I need coverage. Can you hook up a live feed on me? To the entire ship?"

Sylvester rubbed his chin. "Hmmm . . ."

Markham paused with his hands clasped before him, waiting.

"HMMMMM . . ." said Sylvester.

Markham's expression stayed frozen.

"Sylvester!" Nina finally cried.

"Of course I can!" squeaked Sylvester, throwing up his arms. "I'll configure the doohickey right now."

"On a handheld?" said Markham.

"Yessir." Sylvester waved a hand. "One sec . . ."

He disappeared behind a board wall and rummaged in a trunk.

When he returned, he was holding a miniature clay dolphin attached to a neck strap. A little antenna rose from its blowhole. He held it high above his head like a trophy.

"Her name is Lil' Tucuxi."

"Why—?" Markham began, but Nina whacked him with her fist.

"It's lovely," said Nina,

"Lovely?" said Markham. "What the hell is that?"

"An echolocating device," said Sylvester. There was a pause. "Handheld."

Markham covered his face again. "What are we supposed to do with that?"

"I'm glad you asked, squirt. Simply press her dorsal fin like this . . ." Sylvester did so. The dolphin began to vibrate so hard, he had to clasp his other hand around it and hold it out from his body. He raised his now vibrato voice to be heard over the shaking of the device. "And it will send echolocation waves from its nose!" He stopped pressing the dorsal fin. "So long as the antenna is up, and it's pointed at the target, I'll be able to feed sounds and images of your activity to all my stations—radio, TV, and even straight into the minds of any passenger with melon tissue." He flicked the antenna and it blurred.

Markham blinked.

"You take good care of Lil' Tuxy-Wuxy." Sylvester handed it to Nina. "I *knew* you'd come around!" Sylvester turned to Markham and beamed.

Markham leaned over and whispered to Nina. "Are you sure about this?"

She looked down at the strange device in her hands, but her face was thoughtful and confident.

"I trust this," said Nina. "Yes."

Markham sighed. If she trusted it . . .

Sylvester saluted him with a flourish, and Markham pursed his lips.

Then Sylvester hopped back up on his stool and returned to the large camera. "They're ready to get at it again!" he cried.

Markham and Nina looked over at the table once more.

Somehow, one shrimp was on top of the other this time.

"Oh my god," said Markham.

"Mm-mm," Nina shook her head frantically and grabbed his shirt.

A little too interested, Markham craned his head to try and see what was happening on the table. "But how are they—?"

"No." She tugged him back towards the exit.

"I feel really uncomfortable."

Back on the galley level, Markham limped forward with one hand holding the string leash of the frog and the other holding a cane, which was really just a peg leg attached to a broken mop Gavial had found in the pots and pans closet. The little black frog hopped excitedly towards the elevator, leaving inky black tracks on the floor. Nina supported Markham with an arm and glanced over. Lil' Tucuxi was strapped to her back.

"What's uncomfortable?" said Nina.

The frog tried to leap forward and flung back at the tug of the leash like a dog catching a Frisbee. It went for another jump towards the elevator instantly.

"I . . . this?" said Markham. He wobbled along with the broken mop, sighing.

"You look fine." She stared at him long enough to make him look at her. A little innuendo flickered in her eyes, and he smirked and shook his head.

"I'm glad you're attracted to me," he said. "One of these days I'll have to get to know you, too."

The frog reached the lift and tried jumping to slap against what looked like the up button. Markham sighed and punched the button with his thumb. "You sure?" He glared at the little frog, who stared up with big yellow eyes too cute to stomach. "Ugh," said Markham.

Markham tried to share a half smile with Nina, but she wasn't looking at him. He frowned and studied her but jerked to the doors when the lift dinged. The frog tugged on its leash and hopped inside.

To the few purple and pink, gilled passengers slouching along the rail this late in the evening, Markham barked, "Gavial is opening a free midnight buffet. Next ten passengers only."

The passengers exchanged looks and hurried out of the lift, leaving it empty for Markham and Nina. Nina kept her foot at the doors so no one else could call the lift, but her body was tense. She still didn't look at Markham.

"All right, little guy, tell us where," said Markham.

The frog seemed to brace itself. It flattened down as much as it could and then sprang up high—higher than all sixty of the round buttons. It slapped the large circular naval seal at the top.

It landed back on the floor with a splat of black ink. Then it seemed to pant.

Markham's eyebrows pinched together. "What?"

The frog turned its big eyes to Markham in a look that said, *I really have to do that again?*

"Just touch the seal?"

The frog kept its gaze pressed on Markham. Markham blinked, and, with one more glance at the frog, pressed the large naval seal.

Hard.

It rumbled in a few millimeters. Markham pressed hard again. It ground back farther and then slid up into the wall, revealing two square bronze buttons like tablets from an ancient jungle civilization. One had the emblem of the Captain's hat. The one below that had a frog. A socket for the Master Key was beneath both buttons.

"*Ha!*" said Markham. He turned to Nina. "Look!"

Nina, head inclined, glanced over icily before sighing and looking off. Markham and the frog exchanged bewildered glances. He cleared his throat and punched the frog button hard, but it would not budge.

"You have to insert the key first, moron," said Nina.

That was a little harsher than normal. But Markham forced the Master Key into the socket and turned it, creating an echoing *clunk*. He pressed the frog button again, and this time it sank into the wall. Nina withdrew her foot. The doors closed.

Markham took a tender step closer to Nina. "Hey," he said. "You—?"

"What did you mean by that before?" said Nina, leaning on the side of the lift as it began to screech going into the rusty, infrequently used levels of the belly of the ship.

"Wh . . . When?" said Markham, wary.

Nina did a crude impression of Markham's male voice. *"One of these days I'll have to get to know you, too.'"* She gesticulated with her head to make it seem even more ridiculous.

"Nina," Markham moaned. "Come on. I meant . . ."

"You have no idea who I am."

"I—"

"All I am is the first woman you could lay your eyes on out of that tank." She crossed her arms and looked away, a sparkle in her eyes.

"Nina, I don't even know who *I* am!"

"You're the *Captain,* Markham!" Nina spun towards him with a flourish.

Markham mocked that flourish by whisking up his arms. "The Captain! Great! That's all you know about me, too!"

Nina tried to speak, looking appalled.

Markham only nodded with greater heat. "Uh-huh. That's the only reason you were *ever* attracted to me. I was drawn to you right away."

"I . . ." A squeak of sadness entered Nina's tone, as if realizing he might be right. The elevator groaned and jiggled as Markham's lips pressed into a firm line. A dark, uncomfortable feeling crept through his gut, too. He didn't like that he was right either.

Nina looked down at her four-fingered hand and grasped it. Darkness slipped over them as the elevator lost lighting as if diving into an underground tunnel.

"I owed him money," she whispered. "Kloff." A bar of shadow crossed her silhouette.

"I remember," Markham whispered. He was there when those two Kloffers came to warn her at dinner. "But why?"

"I needed a favor."

"Favor?" said Markham.

"I needed to talk to Babsy."

"*What?*" said Markham.

Nina closed her eyes and laid back her head. "You're not the only one who came through the tank, Markham."

Markham's breathing slowed as he watched her. He recalled the shocked way Nina had looked at him, sopping wet, after he'd emerged from the tank . . . the brisk way she knew exactly what he needed to be told to survive . . .

"Many years ago, a baby in a safety pod burst into that tank as well. Gavial fished it out, opened it, and raised it like his own."

"You," said Markham.

Nina nodded. "There was no note, and the pod was only marked with a large wave. Like a tsunami."

Markham blinked. "Do you think you may have come from land somewhere?"

Nina shook her head. "There has never been a land sighting." She looked at Markham. "Ever."

He frowned.

"It obviously came from somewhere underwater," said Nina.

Then Markham remembered the way Nina had looked out his dorm window and dreamed of having a view of the deep blue. She'd seemed almost . . . nostalgic for it.

"Every night," said Nina, "I dream in blue. Just blue. Going on forever."

Markham studied her.

"Babsy lives on the outside hull of the ship," said Nina. "He would've seen where the pod came from."

"Did he?"

Nina blushed. "I was *stupid,* Markham. I don't care how I got here anymore. Kloff probably never even asked Babsy about it for me, but he's been hounding me for his payment ever since. Six months ago, he did this." Nina lifted her maimed hand again. "So that's why he took me again. I ran out of time. He gave me until the end of the year to pay him.

"I've been working for Gavial and feeling like *nothing* and just . . . you came." She wiped her wrist up the bridge of her nose to free herself from tears. Then she looked at him. "You came and I didn't feel like nothing anymore."

"So, you don't know how you got here either." Markham gazed steadily at her.

"No," she whispered.

"You're just as confused."

"Yes," she said. "I've just been confused longer than you."

The elevator began to slow, but Markham didn't take his eyes off her. He spoke with force and urgency. "I have never been more in love with you."

They shook at the stopping of the lift. Nina swallowed and met his gaze.

The doors rumbled open, and they both turned to look out.

Markham's mouth dropped. "Oh my god."

Nina stepped beside him and joined his gaping. "There's no god here, Twenty-Six . . ."

They said the next words together, Markham with a tone of weariness.

"Only the Captain."

TWENTY-SIX

Wide-leafed tropical plants reared along the walls of the hall, and vines tangled together like lovers. Water drizzled from the ceiling and pattered onto glossy lime-and-teal alocasia leaves. Red hibiscus and soft-petaled yellow plumeria painted the green foliage. Birds-of-paradise pointed their tangerine flowers at Markham and Nina like spears.

They moved forward.

The floor beneath them was dark antique tile, gleaming with moisture. Between the jungly foliage perched hundreds of little black frogs, staring at their arrival. The frog on Markham's leash hopped ahead, happy to be home. Totems carved into tiki faces nestled within the plants at the walls and grit their teeth at Markham as he turned to gaze at their cylindrical figures. They seemed to rotate at his passing.

At the end of the hall towered what seemed to be a relief in the wall—a dark, carved-wood panel with ancient writing and images of thresher sharks, atolls, and jackfruit. Torches crackled fire on either end and wavered over the bright shine of wetness everywhere.

Markham breathed in humid air and blinked in astonishment as they approached.

The most interesting of the carvings was one with arrows creating a sequence: frogs, then coal, then steam, then frogs again, as if showing the changing forms of matter. A large, friendly-looking volcano humanoid was carved next to it. It almost looked like a Kloffer. Markham squinted at it.

"Is this a door?" said Nina.

Markham reached out to touch it. The wood was soft. "It's . . ."

"The writing," said Nina. "What does it—?"

"*Makohoni,*" said Markham, scrutinizing the part of the carving his hand touched. "That's what it—"

But at those words, all of the frogs hiding in the plants flooded down from their perches and cartwheeled over one another to come to Markham, ribbiting in an excited riot.

"What?" said Markham, raising his arms and looking around at the crowding at his feet.

Nina laughed and lifted her shoe, which hosted a pair of frogs at its top. "It must mean *you,*" she said.

"*Makohoni?*" said Markham.

The crowd of frogs ribbited louder and leapt up at him like jumping beans. Markham joined in Nina's laughter. "All right," he said. "All right." They settled.

"There's a lot more writing here," said Nina, looking back at the relief. "You can't . . . *read* it, can you?"

Markham's face fell.

. . . Could he?

He stepped closer again.

"*Makohoni*," he said. Nina nodded, watching him apprehensively. His eyes scanned the writing, which was accented with apostrophes and strange curly symbols like waves. "*Is god incarnate.*"

Nina's expression sprang into joy. "You can read it!"

Markham stuttered, dumbfounded. "I . . ." He shook his head. "I kinda *can*. Why?"

Nina jostled his shoulder excitedly. "Keep going!"

With a sigh, Markham leaned forward and squinted again. "*Destined to take the form of a Captain.*" Nina squeezed him. "*Immortal, but slayable, he shall attract the creations to his service.*"

At these words, the frogs started jumping up at him again. His hand fell to sate them.

"*His power . . .*"

His eyes traveled farther, but he did not say more. A worried look crossed Nina's face. "What?" she said. "What does it say?"

Markham moistened his lips and continued to gaze at the relief.

"Markham?"

He met her eyes. "It ends there. The rest is . . . indecipherable. Mildewed."

Nina pursed her lips. "So, you're . . ."

"We don't know that," said Markham. "It's just a carving."

"'*Makohoni*' . . . it rhymes with Markham Brody."

"Spooky," said Markham sarcastically. "Look." He raked a hand through his silver hair. "Let's just . . . find the way into the boiler room."

From the floor, the black frog tied to the leash rolled its big yellow eyes. Markham looked down. "What?" he said. The frog used its eyes to jab a glare at the wooden panel itself. Nina grabbed the sides of the panel with both hands.

"Ha. Wow," she said. "It *is* a door."

"That makes sense," said Markham, relief breathing through his voice.

"Ready?" said Nina, preparing to open it.

"Yeah." Markham straightened his blue Hawaiian shirt with bony-looking petroglyphs and green plantains down the front. One of its coconut-shell buttons was chipped. "Do I look Captainly?"

Nina turned and studied him for an awkward beat. "I'm pretty sure they're going to love you anyway."

"So that's a no," Markham snorted.

Nina grunted. "It's locked," she said.

Markham cursed. "Really?"

A little smile flicked the corner of Nina's lip. In one fluid move, she strode to him and reached for his face.

Markham flinched. "Nina, y—!"

But it was too late. Her lips sunk into his, and he groaned with pleasure, eyes closing. She mussed up his platinum stubble, and he bent his knees to draw her closer against his strong chest. His heart drummed as if wanting to break out and touch her too.

When she pulled back just millimeters, he remained suspended there, not opening his eyes. "I know what I'm doing," she whispered. And he could feel her pull back and look around. A chuckle escaped her breath.

The hall was black with thousands more frogs staring with yellow beacons of eyes up at them.

The carving door had opened.

Together, Markham and Nina turned to it.

Millions. Millions of frogs blackened the enormous, hangar-sized room beyond the door and sat frozen, gaping at them. Huge triple-cylinder steam engines descended in rows into darkness beyond. They seethed steam into the orange atmosphere. They were sixty feet tall, with gigantic piston rods stroking up and down. The overhead set of cylinders on the engines looked like crooked chimneys from a gingerbread house—the lower set out of view.

Pipes and wires gridlocked the ceiling, and below grated bridges and past metal rails were troughs of coal burning so constantly, they looked like lava.

In the center, far, far in the back, was a colossal volcano, covered with staring frogs and coughing out chunk after chunk of rock. The hunks hit the floor somewhere in the distance, and they could hear the echo of them crumbling.

Slowly Markham moved through the door and into the midst of the frogs, whose eyes shifted to stay on him. They shimmied aside at his footfall, and he felt strength—power—surge up from the floor and into his veins.

Behind him, he heard the warble of Nina revving up Lil' Tucuxi. They were live.

Looking around at the millions of frogs bathed in the orange glow, Markham drew in grand breath.

He spoke.

"Makohoni."

He lifted both fists, and the frogs leapt into the air like graduation caps soaring in an auditorium.

PART THREE:

MUTINY

TWENTY-SEVEN

The floor rumbled, and stones trickled down with echoes into the lava.

Heat smudged the air around them, and red glowed on the copper-colored bowels of the volcano.

Markham and Nina lay on their stomachs on a landing inside the volcano, next to spokes and pipes and conveyor belts that squeaked and squeaked like a rusty wheel. The belts emptied coal into the volcano, which caught the coal showers in audible hisses and then bubbled and belched. Little black frogs hopped everywhere with *ribbits,* loading one or two pieces of coal onto each conveyor at a time.

When the steam rose, the grid of piping Markham had seen on the ceiling connected with the top of the volcano and collected the steam, supposedly to feed it into those giant engines. Where all the coal came from—tons and tons required to move this ship indefinitely—Markham had no idea, until he glanced at a pile of coal in the corner he was sure had been frogs only a moment ago . . .

Markham thought back to the sequence carving on the door.

Another slew of frogs lined one of the pipes before Markham and Nina and stared at them expectantly. They wore little yellow construction helmets with executive symbols on the front.

"Okay," said Markham, still on his stomach, for the landing was narrow. "Tell me how to stop this . . . development."

One frog exploded with a *ribbit* ballooning his throat and then continued to stare expectantly at Markham.

A pause.

"I—" said Markham.

"Just say, 'Yes, I'll run your concerns by HR,'" said Nina.

"What?" said Markham.

"He represents a union."

"Yes. I'll run your concerns by HR."

The frog executive jumped off the pipe as if satisfied by this response. The others followed him, and they disappeared into a tiny crack in the side of the landing.

"What!" said Markham. "Where are they going?!"

Nina sighed. "We don't have much time."

"Dammit," Markham hissed, rising carefully to one knee and looking around for a lever, a big red button, anything obvious. Steam rocketed up from the belly of the volcano as a large flood of coal plummeted into it.

Then, just as suddenly, the frogs returned through the crevice and heaved something made of fabric out of the crack.

It was a purple-and-red Hawaiian shirt checkered with

volcanoes, tikis, and palm leaves blazing in a fiery pattern. Mother-of-pearl buttons shimmered down the middle.

All the frogs turned and stared at Markham.

"I'm sorry?" said Markham.

"They would like you to wear the volcano shirt, please," Nina translated.

"Is this the time?" said Markham.

The frogs continued to stare.

"They will not speak to you unless you put on the volcano shirt, Markham."

Now everyone stared at Markham. His mouth hung open.

And then he snatched up the shirt and tugged his current one over his head without even undoing the buttons. The frogs watched, frozen, until every button of the volcano shirt was fastened. Then, only then, one of them ribbited and took off down the ledge. Markham cursed. "Really?" He followed after, watching the tips of his shoes kick off tiny pebbles into the lava below.

Ribbit! The frog's response echoed. Markham huffed and side-stepped through a narrow bend in the volcano. He combed his hands over the rock to quicken his step and keep the hopping black frog in view.

"Stay there, Nina," he called without even looking over his shoulder.

"Are you kidding?" Her voice resounded. "I'm following you with Lil' Tuc—Tux—Lil' Whatever."

"Ugh," said Markham. Agreeing.

He ducked under a low tunnel, and the air around him darkened. His shadow flashed on the wall every few seconds when a mysterious *whoosh* occurred and light exploded into the volcano as its bowels rumbled.

"Yikes," said Nina somewhere behind him.

When at last he stooped out of the tunnel and straightened into the small cave, he breathed a curse of astonishment.

The entire enclosed room was riddled with holes like sideways geysers and aglow in fiery residue.

A podium of spongy black rock stood in the center and held atop it a lever in the shape of a frog. The real frog who'd led him here was sitting at its base and staring expectantly once again at Markham. But just then—

Markham jumped back and flailed his arms. "Wha—!"

Whoosh!

A spitball of lava squirted out of a geyser somewhere on the wall and splattered right at his feet. The ground sizzled.

Again. Another cannonball of lava spat out of a different hole and across the podium. It splashed on the other side of the wall and hung there like mucus before drizzling down.

"How am I supposed to get to the lever?!" Markham actually yelled at the frog.

The frog paused. And then it said, *Ribbit!*

Markham sighed. Nina was at his back, her breath tickling his neck. She shook her head. "Be careful . . ."

He heard the vibration of Lil' Tucuxi and took a single tentative step towards the lever.

Whoosh!

He dove forward and dodged a wad of lava that spattered behind him. Markham's heart jacked into his throat as he glanced at it and crouched there. He licked his lips and rushed forward again.

Whoosh!

Lava singed the silver hairs of his head as he ducked and stumbled off a glossy black slate. He extended an arm. A few more meters and he'd . . .

Markham's eyes flung wide.

"Markham!" cried Nina.

He gasped.

A gob of blazing lava hurtled right for his chest.

"NO!" Nina screamed.

He fell onto his side and cried out in terror as he felt something collide with his shirt. Too late.

He jerked for breath, his eyes tightly closed. The volcano juddered beneath him. He slit open an eye just barely and looked at his chest.

"Ah!"

Lava oozed over his bright Hawaiian shirt. It baked the skin at his neck and warm sweat dripped down his back.

"*Ahhh!*"

He scrambled back. Waiting for his shirt to catch fire.

The frog was there, tugging at his sleeve. Markham jolted towards it.

Ribbit! There was something hard and determined in the little frog's eyes beneath its construction helmet. It glanced at the shirt and then back at Markham.

By the time Markham followed its gaze, the lava on his shirt had slid off and dissolved on the fabric. Markham's mouth dropped.

Whoosh!

Like a comet, another glob of lava wriggled across the air above their heads and made a *splat* somewhere on the other side.

"The volcano shirt," said Markham.

This time the frog executive didn't ribbit but squared its gaze on Markham as if to say, *We're not stupid.*

Markham nodded. He breathed in adrenaline and bravery. "Right."

Whoosh!

Markham ripped to his feet.

He grasped the lever in both hands. Loyally, the frog leapt onto the podium and watched Markham brace his muscles. Rust and molten crumbs crusted the edges of the lever like it had not been touched in millenniums.

Before pulling, Markham shared one last look with the frog. He swallowed. The confidence he'd felt before lifted off him for a moment.

The frog stared deep into him, and intelligence—sympathy, even—illuminated its gaze. For some reason, Markham thought he could understand what the frog meant. *We're in this with you.* It seemed to nod.

Markham closed his eyes. He heaved the lever back.

It didn't budge. The cave quaked with the rumbles of the volcano. *Whoosh!*

Markham's face twisted in effort. He shined with sweat. Another pull with all his might . . .

Whoosh!

The lever cracked through just a centimeter of the debris locking it stiff. Markham lurched with the jolting of the cave but continued to pull.

Whoosh! Whoosh! Whoosh!

As if the volcano knew what Markham was doing, it belched out twice as many patties of lava and tossed them into every corner like a mad artist hurling paint. Dollops splashed onto Markham's shirt, and the cave screeched and snarled as lava combusted into fires all around him.

Markham roared. The frog glanced worriedly at the lever and jumped onto Markham's shoulder. It turned and fired out its tongue, grasping hold of the lever with it, then closed its eyes and pulled with him.

Crack!

The lever snapped back.

Markham stumbled onto his back.

Like a rattling furnace, the volcano shook and seethed for a few more seconds and then . . .

Energy drained from the cave. The whooshing stopped. Conveyor belts began audibly droning to a halt. Only spoonfuls of lava continued to drip off the geysers in the walls.

Finally . . . the vibrating on the ground beneath Markham ceased.

The volcano's dying breath.

TWENTY-EIGHT

"What if they still don't believe us? How would they know I'm not just some guy who found his way down there?" Markham leaned his forehead on the elevator wall and twirled the Master Key in his hands below him as the lift rose from the depths. The elevator was still in its rocky, rattling phase, not yet up to the smooth common floors of the ship.

"*And* commanded the frogs?" said Nina. "I got it *all* on echolocation, Markham. And even if there are some doubters, you ended the *Great Turn!* They'll want to *elect* you Captain after that!" Nina, hair windswept and singed black from the hot breath of the volcano, tapped her finger lovingly against the head of a tiny black frog in her palm. It stared ahead contentedly, its big eyes seeming to pulse larger every time Nina squeezed him.

"Do you think this is a recognizable Captain relic?" Markham pinched the fireproof magenta-and-red Hawaiian shirt the frogs had given him.

"No, I think that's hideous," said Nina, looking down nonchalantly at the frog and continuing to stroke it. "Sorry," she added. "Usually I like your Hawaiian shirts."

The elevator began to hum a sweet, smooth tone. They'd entered the commons of the ship.

"I just—why do you still have a frog?" Markham hit the wall with an exasperated fist and turned to her.

Nina covered the frog with her other hand and shielded it away from Markham. "Don't scare him."

"Nina, *I'm* scared. What if—?"

The elevator dinged. Faster than Markham expected. They turned to it.

Markham's mouth dropped. "Oh no."

They were at the dining hall. And in the center of overturned tables and chairs sparkled the shattered remains of . . .

The giant chandelier.

The lights were cut, and the room was nearly black, but golden wine reflected in the chandelier's glass. Spots of white also still pulsed in the candleholders that were angled every which way on the ground. Along the walls, Markham could make out long claw gashes.

Nina grasped Markham's arm as they moved out onto the floor.

"Gavial?" Nina called out tentatively.

"Something happened h—" Markham turned his head up to the echo of a shout somewhere from all the floors that towered above them. He focused his ears: thumps of rushing footsteps somewhere distant, more cries . . .

He stumbled back and gaped at the shadowed railings of the

ascending floors. In the waver of torchlight, red banners with enormous *K*'s hung from the first three decks. More shouting and clanging reverberated down the atrium, its source clearer now: the fourth deck.

"Nina," said Markham. He swallowed. "I want you to understand that they're fighting Kloff. He's taken over the first three floors, including the one we're standing on, which means—"

"Which means we have to *go,*" said Nina, and she pushed Markham with both hands towards the kitchen. She dropped the tiny frog, and it hopped back to the safety of the elevator.

Someone above emitted a gurgling cry. A hunk of shadow soared down the dark air into the atrium and bumped off an overturned table. It rolled on the floor in front of Markham and Nina's feet and into the pulsating light of a candleholder . . .

A large, severed fish head with cornflower blue scales and death-stricken wide eyes. The smallest bowler hat in the world was on its top.

"Oh my god!" Nina jumped.

"Fish or person?!" said Markham.

"Oh my god!"

"FISH OR PERSON?!?!" Markham yelled.

"BOTH!" cried Nina. "GO!" She shoved him into the kitchen. "They're killing passengers!"

Just then, Gavial's tall, powerful silhouette covered the entire doorway of his kitchen, as if he was waiting for them to enter. His white chef jacket was stained with brownish-red spots. His toothless jaw was open, and his eyes were sharp and electric with fight. The shaky light carved his reptilian features, making him scary for the first time since Markham had come to know his jovial heart.

Even before Nina could declare Gavial's name in relief, his throat bobbed and grumbled.

Nina nodded.

"What did he say?" said Markham.

"He said Kloff was enraged you ended the Great Turn and ordered his men to take the decks with bloodshed."

"I can see," Markham panted. He held up the Master Key to Gavial. "What do I do?"

Gavial gave a snarl so uncharacteristic of him that shivers hitched up the hairs on the back of Markham's neck.

"He says to put that away," Nina said. "He says it's time."

Markham turned to Nina with alarm. "For what? *Time for what, Nina?*"

Gavial's claws clasped Markham's shoulders.

"To go," Nina translated. "To put you away, protect you. Babsy is trying to drill into the ship and hunt you, Markham."

"Gavial!" said Markham.

Gavial began to lift Markham into his arms, but Markham shouted with thunderous authority. "*STOP!*"

Gavial froze and pinned him with urgent black eyes.

Markham swallowed hard.

"I'm not going into hiding. If Babsy and Kloff want me, let them come. My ship is in danger." He paused, and his chest grew with breath. "I know what I need to do."

Gavial continued to stare at Markham, calculating. His reptilian muscles rippled . . . and then loosened.

Gavial nodded.

"Take me to my parlor," ordered Markham.

Like an obedient shipmate, Gavial hoisted Markham into his arms.

Nina leapt at Gavial's heels as the crocodile dashed for the vent that Crocidius had pulled them into not long before.

"Nina," said Markham, over Gavial's shoulder. "I want you to—"

"NO, MARKHAM!" Nina said. "I'M NOT LETTING YOU GO AHEAD. I'LL FIGHT! I'LL F—!"

"Duh!" said Markham. "I was going to say hold this!" He threw her the Master Key. She caught it.

Gavial stuffed Markham into the dark metal vent. Markham clanked onto the steel insides, then scrambled around to see them. "Why not the elevator?" he said.

"The elevator won't work," Nina translated as Gavial grunted. "Kloff's men would shoot it. He's expecting you."

Gavial's expression softened as he turned to Nina and gently drew her into his arms. Fatherly love glowed on his face as he closed his eyes. Nina held him tight. Then he prepared to lift her up after Markham.

"So how are we—?!"

Gavial chirped.

"This will take you to the top," Nina translated.

"The top?! Through here?" On his hands and knees, Markham pivoted to look down the moist dark tunnel in the ceiling he was in. He moved to make room for Nina.

"Yes," she panted.

And then Gavial coiled his mighty back legs and leapt up in one lithe movement. He slipped inside the vent on his belly.

Another two chirps.

"Grab him," said Nina. "And hold on."

"God help me." Markham climbed atop Gavial's back and gripped his craggy green horns tight.

"Talking to yourself now?" said Nina as he bunched her up in his other arm. And then Gavial's stumpy legs battered the metal floor of the vent with hollow *clanks*, and he shot forward into the blackness.

The ride was so bumpy that at one point Markham hit his head and winced, but Gavial knew his way exactly. He scaled steps with urgency, jumping through the maze of tunnels hidden in the walls of the ship that only Gavial and Crocidius seemed to know how to navigate. Markham and Nina squeezed the crocodile more firmly as he continued. Up. They were definitely, gradually, climbing *up*.

"WHERE," Markham shouted over the metallic bangs of their passage, "IS CROCIDIUS?"

This will be the tell, thought Markham. Did Crocidius betray them and finally start fighting for Kloff?

"WAITING FOR YOU!" translated Nina. "HE BELIEVES YOU'LL COME, JUST LIKE EVERYONE ELSE DOES."

"IS THAT WHY KLOFF ATTACKED?" said Markham.

"YES. THEY FINALLY BELIEVE YOU'RE—"

Gavial turned right into a blast of light and tumbled out of the wall. A rush of cool air and oxygen blew over them as Gavial curled and landed on his side on the floor. Markham and Nina ricocheted off him.

Markham's shoes squeaked as he ripped to his feet. *Squeaked.* He knew that squeak.

With breath pounding in and out of him like the batter of waves against the hull, he wheeled around to survey the surroundings.

The Captain's Parlor.

Gavial had made it there.

Those floor-to-ceiling windows splashed menacing grey light on the polished rose marble—outside, fittingly, lightning forked over dark clouds and the ocean spiked up and down.

No one fought on this deck, but cries of rage and agony pierced their ears from immediately below, just past the open railing of the parlor. Torchlight even threw tall, distorted shadows onto the curtains. Figure tackling figure. Blunt and bladed objects being lifted over heads. Hands and fins rising to stop it. Kloff may have only won the first three decks at the moment, but skirmishes were now breaking out everywhere.

Markham bolted to the parlor railing and looked down at the open decks tiered out below.

Yes. Blood—green, red, and blue—pooled at the floor and swirled into dirty hues of vomit-brown and soulless grey. The battle was a strange clash of humanoid and oceanic. Harpoons impaled fishlike bodies that wriggled and flapped. The pearl farmers Markham encountered before knocked scantily-clothed Kloffers over the head with rakes.

The alien faces and bodies of both gangster and passenger overwhelmed Markham as he squeezed the railing with white knuckles. Emotion swung through him, almost hurled him over the side and into the bloody throng. Somehow, beyond his comprehension and into the primordial, these were his people. Weeping, bleeding, dying. And the Kloffers were clearing the floor.

Markham shook his head.

He spun to Gavial behind him.

The squelch of blades into bodies continued below. Markham lowered his voice.

"I need a bat."

Gavial, standing upright again, reached into his chef jacket. His black eyes clutched Markham's as he pulled out a three-foot wooden oar and the dry-erase/blackboard and held out the oar to Markham. Markham read the board.

I hoped you would.

Markham blinked with surprised approval. He didn't expect Gavial to heed his demand that readily. Then Markham nodded and took the heavy oar—more fitting than a bat, he reasoned— his brows hard on his face.

He looked ahead.

Firelight flashed on the glass case of the Captain's uniform.

Gavial gurgled.

"It's time," Nina whispered to Markham, translating.

Goosebumps erupted over him. *It's time.*

Markham gripped the oar hard in his fist. He moved for the case.

One last time, standing before it, Markham stared into his firelit reflection for a whole beat. The hat reflected over his silver hair; the gold buttons glimmered down his front. He breathed in and the navy coat's powerful shoulders seemed to rise with his.

Markham drew back the oar, strode forward, and roared.

The oar crashed into the glass. Fragments exploded into the air and rained down onto the floor, then bounced like a thousand marbles. Glass tore into Markham's hands, and he flung the oar across the floor, where it slid and whirled like a spinning bottle.

Nina was there, taking the heavy Captain's coat off the mannequin. Gavial lifted off the white hat.

"Here, baby," Nina whispered at his side. Markham dove his arm through the sleeve, and she jerked the coat over his back as he dipped in his other arm. The weight of the fabric was cool. Familiar.

Right.

He buttoned his anchor-embellished gold buttons down his front, the thick sleeves bunching at the gold-striped cuffs.

Gavial set the Captain's hat down upon Markham's silver hair. Already Markham wore the shiny black dress shoes they'd found in the cabin.

Lastly, Nina drew the green sand dollar amulet with the anchor crest over his head.

This is it, he thought. If he wasn't the Captain, he recalled Nina saying, the burn of the Captain's amulet would nearly kill him.

He touched it to his chest and looked at them.

It didn't burn.

It belonged to him.

The Captain.

They froze and looked at Markham. Tears streamed down Nina's face.

"Now go," she whispered. Pointing to the rail.

Markham turned. With precise steps that still managed to echo on the marble floor, he approached the rail once more.

Gavial scurried on his stomach to the other end of the rail and rose, signaling with a dinosaur-like call and wave of his hand to something on the other side of the atrium, many decks below. Markham glanced at Gavial and then in the direction he was indicating. Another super-tall shadow that could belong to no one but Crocidius rose across the atrium. He waved a claw as well from his far away deck, and then . . .

Light burst onto Markham in a beam. He winced and started to raise a hand but stopped. Instead, he glared into the blinding shine and placed one foot on the rail's rung.

He climbed it.

Weapons dropped on the open deck below him.

"IT CAN'T BE!"

"IT'S HIM!"

"THE CAPTAIN FROM THE ECHOLOCATION!"

"NOOOOO!" Kloffers cried.

Markham balanced himself on the soles of his dress shoes on the railing. He held out his arms, swaying in the spotlight.

A god towering over his people.

Passengers—crowds of hundreds—stumbled back in awe. They stopped and laid back their heads. Mouths hung open.

The light Crocidius shone at him struck his epaulettes, his cuffs, buttons, the leaves crawling along his black visor. It highlighted his silver hair and stubble and fiery blue eyes. Markham closed his hands into fists.

He raised his arms out over his head.

TWENTY-NINE

Markham bent his knees to jump from the balcony and into the crowd of battle. A hand hooked the collar of his Captain's jacket and reeled him back.

"Not so fast, Captain Crunch."

He staggered onto the floor and into Nina's arms. The spotlight glaring on his gold buttons cut to black, and Markham blinked the spots of light from his eyes. Gavial snarled in the shadows next to them.

"You've chummed the waters," said Nina. "They're gonna target you like a beached whale now."

Gavial chirped. He held the oar out in both hands, having retrieved it from the floor. He left the whiteboard on the ground.

"Give me that," said Markham, snatching the oar from Gavial. "What do you suggest?"

"Well, that went live," said Nina, patting Lil' Tucuxi. "Everyone not in the fight for you yet will be now. We need to help them take back the ship."

Gavial clucked and pointed in the direction of the spotlight, many decks down.

"Right," said Nina. "You need to fight with your passengers, but you need a guard. Gavial wants us to meet up with Crocidius. They'll keep the poison darts off you."

"Metaphorically speaking?" said Markham.

Thud!

A dart trembled on the balcony post where Markham had been standing in the spotlight.

"Nope," said Nina. "Let's go!"

Gavial seized Markham, and his jasmine scent filled Markham's head before he could protest. Then Gavial took one heavy step forward and punted him over the edge of the balcony and onto the stage of the fifty-ninth deck.

Markham bowled into a pair of sparrers. All three fell down and rolled along the floor.

A monstrous, lionlike roar boomed into the room as Gavial dropped onto the lower deck on two feet. Markham rolled to his side to see, his Captain's hat tilted over one eye. He shoved a sleeve up to balance it, unused to the weight of the uniform. Kloffers and muddy-looking pirates jumped on Gavial all at once, sabers raised. Gavial roared again and flung them off him like he was flinging monkeys off a giant tree.

Bodies flashed around Markham, blades making a *ting!* at every turn. Nina was there, grabbing his lapels. Markham hopped to his feet, oar still in hand.

"You okay?" breathed Nina.

A grey, slime-oozing Kloffer with two eyepatches crept up behind Nina, dagger in fist. Markham shoved Nina aside and gripped the oar with both hands, hurling his entire back into the swing across its face. *Crack!* The alien-looking Kloffer's neck snapped, and it crashed to the floor, writhing like a beheaded snake.

Markham nodded and then stared at her, shoulders heaving with breath. Flushed, she returned the gaze, and for a powerful beat, it felt like they would kiss and grapple.

"Screw it," said Markham. He dove to collide his mouth against hers for just a second.

She threw her arms around his neck, and he tore back an instant later.

An audience of tiny black frogs surrounded them and stared, indifferent to the war around them. Markham's mouth hung open, and he nodded, this time grateful for their reliable and paranormal interest in his romantic relations.

He raised the oar with one arm.

"FIGHT!" Markham ordered. The frogs began to glance around. Once they identified the gangsters quarrelling with passengers, they hopped in every which direction like rain pellets bouncing off asphalt. Triangular-shaped, lava-dripping Kloffers gave the frogs double takes and stumbled backwards as the frogs leapt onto their skin and covered their eyes. The Kloffers screamed and fell.

Gavial bumped Markham with his rough green snout, and they moved onward, feet slapping hardwood and then treading over the patterned brown carpet of the hallway. Keypads on dormitory doors continued to blink red light onto the deck's railing, which trailed all around the atrium where the elevator once operated.

Dark lumps—both passenger and gangster—lay on the floor in patches, haloed with blood.

Markham, Gavial, and Nina veered into the empty staircase and thundered down it for ten minutes, turning at each flight so fast Markham's head spun until finally Gavial cut into a hallway nearly forty floors below, under the sign that read Deck Twenty.

Ahead, and around the curve of the rail where the spotlight had shone from, Markham caught sight of the tall, crooked silhouette of Crocidius. He fought against gangsters in a similar fashion to Gavial, ripping off attackers like they were jungle vines. His long jaw snapped in the air with a loud *clap!*

They weaved through a thicker population of battlers towards Crocidius. It looked like Kloff had won more decks, flags hanging into the atrium only seven floors below.

They tried to push their way up. Gavial bobbed up and down from a four-legged run to a quick rise-and-slash with his claws on any thug trying to reach Markham. Markham mimicked this, striking the oar over the heads of anyone he could smite without slowing down.

They reached Crocidius at the wide lobby next to the opposite stairwell. He was feral and nightmarish, tongue black and wagging out as he swept assailants away with his massive claw. Saliva seethed from his teeth. His black eyes bulged with fire.

Stationed at the railing behind him was an anglerfish the size of a small car. A lightbulb dangled from a long stem attached to its forehead. Some odd lampshade steadied its bulb and pointed it at the Captain's Parlor far up and across the atrium where Markham had stood. The anglerfish's gills flared, and its eyes were big and blank, mouth open.

This had been the spotlight.

Past the anglerfish was a large, framed oil painting of someone with a hump on his back. He wore a trench coat and held a cane with his twisted hand. The plaque on the frame named him the Flying Hunchman. The portrait was positioned next to a banana tree plant—both accents to the little lobby.

Gavial called to Crocidius in reptilian. Crocidius swung his head towards them. His eyes fell on Markham while Gavial spoke in a hopeful, explanatory tone. Markham studied Crocidius hard, continuing to hook the brown crocodile's gaze.

Though begrudgingly, it seemed, Crocidius' breath evened. He appeared to accept becoming Markham's second guard. It seemed like he wouldn't be killing him after all.

Seemed.

Markham nodded once and then surveyed the area.

The amount of times Gavial or Crocidius snarled and struck lessened. Kloffers seemed to retreat down empty halls and into shadows.

"They're turning the tide, Markham," said Nina. "We're doing it!"

Crocidius clicked out a clearly snide remark.

"He says Kloff tried to air photos of when they forced a Kloff shirt on you in your bed."

Markham couldn't remember, but assumed the Kloffers had pinned him down and tugged the shirt over him while he was sleeping. According to the images that flashed in his mind during the drinking game in the casino, he must have wriggled free shortly after and fought. And that must have been just before they cornered him to the balcony of his quarters . . .

"The attempt didn't work," said Nina. "We clearly got the better ratings."

Markham's heart darkened, however. That meant someone somewhere was holding a gun to Sylvester's head.

"This isn't over," said Markham. "I know he's—"

"YOUUUUUUUS COWARD!!!"

All four of them flinched at the familiar voice. They approached the railing next to the anglerfish and looked down.

There was Kloff, standing on the top of the dysfunctional cabled elevator like a yellow war elephant. He held a six-foot harpoon in hand and a skirt of palm leaves covered him. Cuts trailed down his ugly face. He shook a fist, which made his arm fat flap.

"FACE ME, CAPTAIN!" he bellowed to the ship at large. Thundering footsteps and cries still echoed from the lower balconies, but the ones above, like where Markham stood now, quieted, and Captain-loyal passengers rushed downstairs to reinforce the fighters near the bottom, where Kloff fought to keep his thirteen won decks.

"It's over," Markham breathed. He looked down the atrium at the Captain-loyal troops flooding out the Kloffers. "He's—"

The floor jutted, and windows, glass, and wood panels shook.

They froze.

With another *boom*—like the ominous stomping of a giant approaching—Markham reached out to the rail for support.

He looked at Nina darkly. "What is that?"

And then—

BOOM!

Wood boards and the oil painting blasted apart.

A jet of water swept Markham off his feet and he hit the ground as the white seawater crashed over him. A stream of bubbles burst from his mouth as he clamped a hand to his hat to keep it from escaping. It felt just like the beginning of this all, when he was flushed underwater and into the kitchen pipes. The water shocked his heartbeat with cold. Salt stung his tongue and eyes.

He couldn't pull himself up. The current kept battering, and now it forced him back, it made him tumble over himself until he hit the railing and started to slip through . . .

A powerful hand grabbed Markham's arm. It hauled him out of the current and into oxygen. Markham gasped and shivered. The roar of crashing water reverberated in the room now, like a waterfall in a wide cave. It began to cascade over the rail and into the atrium.

Crocidius was holding him with his one hand, but the water pounded against his back too, and it seemed to take all the strength the crocodile had to hang there. He coughed and his eyes bulged.

Still grasping Markham, Crocidius turned them to the puncture in the wall. Stepping through the gush of ocean water were five skeletal pink legs. Two enormous pinchers held a wide shotgun with a harpoon-bayonet attached to the barrel. Bright red eyes, which illuminated like glowsticks, blinked atop long stems. The crab carried a jagged black shell on its back with barnacles and plastic soda-can rings attached to it. Other coral-ridden, barnacle-covered, moss-coated beings sloshed onto the deck. They dragged severed prison chains along their wrists or ankles.

The crab's eyes found Crocidius and Markham. Its black whiskers formed a mustache and ticked like insect antennae.

"Crocidius . . ." Its voice was scratchy, low, and exaggerated. It didn't fit, as if it had hired someone scarier and deeper to speak through its mask.

Crocidius growled and bared his teeth.

When the crab turned to wave in more troops, Markham saw the *B* on its shotgun.

Babsy.

"I thought you'd come around," Babsy said to Crocidius. "Now drop him." His whiskers ticked in the direction of Markham.

Crocidius hunched all his muscles, eyes darkening. Markham wasn't sure what that meant.

"Or will you both just let your love drown?" said Babsy. He looked calmly down into the water before them. Nina's dark silhouette blurred in the rush of froth. She was stuck under the current, beneath the anglerfish's tail.

Crocidius' brow jumped, and he rammed his great shoulder into the anglerfish. The light from the fish's bulb swung and highlighted the foam of the water, and its heavy flesh lifted just enough for Nina to free herself.

Just like Markham, she started to slip right through the rail. Her hands swished out to grab support.

"Get her!" said Markham.

Too late. Nina's warbling scream could be heard as she plummeted over the railing with the waterfall.

"NO!" Markham reached out a hand.

Over by the stairwell, Gavial popped out of the water, showering droplets into the white current. He called for Crocidius with a watery cough-honk, still hacking out water from his throat. Had he seen Nina fall over the side?! He beckoned for their retreat, but Crocidius couldn't move without untangling his feet from the rail and losing grip of Markham.

Babsy's whiskers seemed to turn up and his legs churned through the water with ease.

"That's the end of that love triangle," said Babsy. "Now to take this ship." He aimed his shotgun at Markham.

Gavial's roar spiked the air next to them. He leapt onto Babsy.

Crocidius closed his eyes and tried to heave Markham up—but he had no other hand to help pull, and even with his colossal strength, the blast of water at his back was strong enough to capsize a U-boat.

Markham reached up his other hand and clapped it onto Crocidius' rough skin. "You can do it, Crocidius," he grunted. The water was spraying into his eyes. Crocidius' half-torn black sand dollar amulet brushed his face.

"DOOOOOOOON'T WORRY! I GOT HER!"

Crocidius opened his eyes. He locked them with Markham, who was equally horrified. That was Kloff's voice, from the top of the suspended elevator.

Markham strained over his shoulder to follow Crocidius' gaze.

Kloff hung from the cable of the elevator, which the waterfall struck against and rolled off in sheets.

In his hand, Nina squirmed and batted her fists.

"NINA!" Markham shouted.

Kloff rumbled with laughter that echoed with the loud keen of the waterfall. "THANKS FOR THE SNACK, BABSY!" he boomed up the decks. He didn't see Gavial and Babsy biting and clawing in the water, though Gavial's toothless gums just slipped across Babsy's shell. "I'LL BE SURE TO THROW HER BACK UP WHEN I'M DONE."

He flopped Nina over his shoulder and began to descend the elevator to reach for the nearby rail of a lower deck.

Markham flailed and cried. "NO!" Tears mixed with the salt of the sea. "NOOO!!!"

Crocidius matched his howls.

Then, before Markham could realize what he would do, Crocidius barked an angry curse.

The crocodile untangled his feet from the railing.

"Wait," said Markham. "Wait!"

Too late.

Crocidius dove over the railing for Nina.

He released his grasp, and Markham fell.

THIRTY

Thwack! Gavial smacked Babsy's harpoon-bayonet onto the railing and fired down at Markham. The spearhead and rope slithered down the waterfall.

Markham swatted for it in freefall. He tossed it between his hands and then grabbed hold. Heat burned down his palms as they skidded down the material. Bones cracked in his hands as he twisted his ankles together and jolted to a halt. The rope creaked and rocked like a pendulum with his weight and the water splashing down on it.

Gavial, brown-red blood streaking down his face, slapped one claw over another and reeled Markham up to the balcony again. He clawed Markham's back and hauled him over, keeping his digits clenched on Markham's sopping, heavy jacket.

Gavial clucked and whimpered something Markham couldn't

understand. He led Markham through the strong current to the stairwell. Babsy was nowhere in sight.

In the shelter of the stairwell, the current was softer, only burbling down the staircases like a brook over stones. Gavial released Markham, and Markham fell at the wall and sobbed dryly.

"*Nina*," he moaned.

Gavial clucked fiercely.

With eyes bloodshot from both grief and salt, Markham turned his head and studied Gavial. Gavial watched him furiously as the water rose past their ankles. He clearly wanted Markham to understand as he repeated his clicks and throat bobs.

"Can you write?" Markham said thickly, before remembering the whiteboard lying there on the parlor floor.

Gavial flapped open his white chef jacket in one harsh gesture to show he didn't have the whiteboard and jerked it closed again. His eyes didn't tear away from Markham.

"What do you want me to do?!"

Gavial sloshed through the water at him and laid both hands over Markham's shoulders.

He gazed into Markham's eyes the way he had when Markham first flipped over the rim of the tank in the kitchen. Markham swallowed, his heart pattering with a little of that old fear. But he tried to look back. Listen.

Comprehend.

He wore the goddamn Captain's hat. He was the *Captain*.

Gavial clucked.

Markham blinked.

Cluck. Gurgle. Hummm.

Markham's brow lowered.

Cluck. Gurgle.

Cluck. You.

Gurgle.

Understood.

Hummmmmm.

Once.

Markham's mouth dropped.

"I understood once," he breathed.

Gavial's eyes swiveled to every corner of Markham's features. His jaw slackened, and his expression brightened.

Understand again, Captain Brody.

Markham drew shaky breath. "We have to get Nina."

No. Crocidius will rescue her surer than either of us could. Babsy's reinforcements—

"Slow down," said Markham.

Okay. He slowed. *Babsy's reinforcements will slay your passengers quickly. They are professional killers.*

"What happened to Babsy?" Markham pinched his eyes to clear the saltwater that dripped into them from his hair. "Did you fight him off?"

I disarmed him and he shelled himself and rolled away towards the lower levels. They will claim the decks above Kloff's rapidly.

"So we'll go down and fight them," said Markham. "We don't stop until they're all dead."

You will not win. Those loyal to you will fall.

"Then what?" Markham snapped back. The water rose another centimeter up his pant legs.

Recruit those not loyal to you.

"You mean the ones down there slaughtering my passengers?" Markham pointed down the staircase. "Recruit them on my side?"

The ones loyal to neither.

"What?"

Obensteen.

Markham blinked. And then nodded. "Obensteen." He remembered the entire casino full of Obensteen's followers. "How? Will he join me?"

You'll convince him.

"I thought no one knows who he is. How do I even find him?"

You once knew.

"Okay, well!" Markham threw his arms up. "I'm talking to a crocodile, that's enough of a breakthrough in one day!"

Think.

Markham did. The sound of gushing water filled his ears and rang through nothing but emptiness.

"I don't remember," he stated.

Gavial blew warm breath from his nostrils and slumped.

"I'm sorry," said Markham.

Then who would know?

"Even Obensteen's men don't know," replied Markham. "And no one knows more than I."

Except your confidant.

"Nina?"

Someone who has known you longer.

"You?"

You always preferred me in the kitchen.

"God, Gavial just say it!"

Gavial seemed to flick an eyebrow.

Your First Mate.

Markham punched his hand with a fist. "Yastley."

Gavial was silent for a beat. And then he nodded. Markham mirrored him.

"Time to break him out."

Stretchers charged through the bright white hospital lobby, and doctors ripped aside curtains on plastic rings to usher them into operating rooms. The smell of antiseptics and fresh bandages stung the air.

All within the lobby, patients were piled and stacked. On beds, across the floor . . . anywhere there was space, and in some places there wasn't. The reception desk was empty as nurses holding pillows and painkillers combed about the limbless, unconscious, half-dead passengers. Some of the wounded were hooked to oxygen, others, a bubbling tank of filtered saltwater. They varied from scaled and fishlike to humanoid to invertebrate. One or two even wore an old, tarnished Mariner uniform—Mariner loyalists creeping from hiding into the battle. The ladybug Markham had seen on his first day aboard was on its back with its wings torn off.

The parrot still perched in its cage behind the reception desk.

"WAWK! WHAT"RE WE GONNA DO! WAWK!"

Breath slipped from Markham. Overwhelmed by the pain.

He moved in among the patients.

Faces turned. Eyes twitched open beneath soiled bandages.

"It's . . . him."

"The Cap . . ."

"And Gavial. Alive."

Voices lifted up to them from the floor. Shaky hands reached out for Markham's hems. Markham stopped at each arm, touching them. Others brushed his back, his shoes. Sobs of joy began to ring in the lobby.

One man, so wrapped in gauze that he resembled a mummy, coiled his arms around Markham's neck. Markham bent over him and embraced him gently and wordlessly, eyes closed.

The nurses stopped in their tracks. Those who could cheered and applauded. The praise grew louder.

"HE LIVES!"

"THE CAPTAIN!"

Markham straightened from the bandaged man.

"I'm alive," he said. "I'm with you."

It was all he could formulate.

It was all they needed.

Nurses and doctors rushed up to him and, with tears, patted him, kissed him.

"Your Helmsman," a doctor breathed.

"Captain," a nurse said. "What do you need? How can we—?"

Markham, realizing the power of his touch, braced his hands on the nurse's shoulders and looked into her eyes.

"I need you to take me to First Mate Yastley."

A pause. The nurses and doctors exchanged wary looks.

"Yes, Captain," the doctor said. Still cautious. "Immediately."

The doctor led the way, cutting through the maze of stretchers. Markham strode after her confidently. He was beginning not to notice the weight of the Captain's hat on his head. Gavial followed in his wake. The hospital was deep, cries and moans muffled past every curtained-off room and down every polished white hallway until the doctor punched buttons on a lock pad and opened a door.

This hallway had dirty cement floors rather than white tile. The ceiling was open to foam and pipes, one of which leaked onto the ground, creating a murky black puddle.

A locked metal door faced them.

The doctor turned to Markham and handed him the key. "He was . . . biting the nurses. I realize he's the First Mate, but with the overload of patients, I—"

Markham put up a hand. He took the key. "Understood."

The doctor nodded, glanced once at the door, and rushed back to the lobby of patients.

Markham moved into the dingy hallway and plunged the key into the metal door. It jingled. He pulled it open and entered.

Just like the cell Kloff had confined Yastley to, the room was windowless and steel. A single white bed sat in the corner, Yastley sleeping on it. He wore his white First Mate uniform with silver epaulettes and buttons. It had been respectfully dry-cleaned and ironed. On the nightstand were strange electric machines, lie detectors, and monitors that must have been designed to reverse the effects of torture Kloff had used to render Yastley speech-impaired. A blood pressure cuff was hooked to Yastley's ankle.

A light machine on the nightstand emitted soothing images of flying pelicans and lighthouses, glowing and rotating all around the walls.

Gavial stayed at the doorway. Markham's footsteps clanked as he approached Yastley's bed. He touched Yastley's chest and stood there, waiting for him to wake.

Yastley twitched, and then he stirred and looked up at Markham there in his full, uniformed Captain glory. Yastley's tongue and mouth wiggled with excitement and the attempts of speech.

"C—"

Markham laid a hand on Yastley's cheek.

"Cap . . ."

Markham nodded. "Captain Brody," Markham said. Stroking Yastley's cheek.

Yastley grinned. Tears swirled in his eyes.

"I need your service once again," said Markham.

Yastley ripped off the pressure cuff and leapt out of bed. Markham stepped back in alarm.

The First Mate lunged onto Markham with a tearful hug. Markham grunted, still a little disarmed, and then he squeezed Yastley into his coat for a long beat. Markham thumped him on the back.

"I know you can't speak," said Markham, drawing back at last. "So." A pause. Markham studied Yastley to see if he really had this task in him. There was a hard and sure look in Yastley's eyes now.

Markham nodded. "Take me to Obensteen."

THIRTY-ONE

Markham looked down at the atrium. White-clothed tables floated, and silverware flashed off the bottom like ore in a river. More water driveled off every balcony from the twentieth deck—where the hull puncture was—and down with the patter of a dozen rainforest waterfalls. The battle noise now echoed like the space in an indoor pool.

Markham had to force himself not to look around. Not to be tugged aside by the sight of a club striking a passenger's head or a crony of Kloff or Babsy cackling in the distance like they were in some nightmarish haunted carnival.

Yastley was rocketing for the stairwell on the other side of the deck. Markham and Gavial kept pace, occasionally touching hands to the railway on the edge of the hall.

The First Mate dove up the stairs.

Deck 26. Twenty-seven. Yastley knew exactly where he was going. He bypassed the number signs without even looking up.

At Deck 29, Yastley turned and fell on his hands and knees in haste, speeding onto the deck.

"What's on twenty-nine?" Markham asked Gavial.

Gavial growled in reply—at least that was all Markham heard this time.

War still waged on this deck, but all of Babsy's prisoners lined the balcony over the atrium, shaking their arms above their heads. Broken chains rattled from their wrists. Some wore helmets filled with saltwater like the squid-gun-wielding assassins had had. Their backs were to Markham.

He strained to see what they were hooting at.

Ropes fell from the upper deck and hung there wiggling. One of Babsy's men climbed the rail and grabbed a rope, cutlass in hand. He stepped off the rail and swung through the air. Across the atrium, a Captain-loyal passenger—a walrus-man with a bowtie and one broken tusk—did the same on another rope. In midair, they clashed blades and swung past each other. More sport than skirmish. Babsy's pirates hollered and jumped as the walrus rocked up near them.

Cannon fire rumbled from several decks above. Shards of wood showered the atrium.

Markham's heart pounded. Every second was another injury. He huffed to keep up with Yastley, who passed the lobby and sped down a hallway of residences—dorm numbers and porthole windows flashing by their periphery.

Markham started to recognize the style of the hallway.

Yastley cut sharply left and disappeared from view. When Markham turned after him, he saw the descending grated staircase that had become so familiar. Smooth white hallway at the bottom. One watertight door on the right with spokes for a handle and a claw-footed tub icon.

The sauna.

Markham hammered down the grated stairs and met Yastley at the sauna door. Gavial pounded down after him.

The fresh smell of chlorine seeped through the door. Steam fogged the porthole window into the dim sauna.

"Here?" Markham looked at Yastley, disbelieving. Yastley stared back fiercely. "*Here?*" Markham bounced on his heels and shook his fists. *This* can't *be,* he thought. *How's Obensteen in the sauna at a time like this?*

Yastley nodded again. Something so wanting, so sweet and loyal, swam in the First Mate's eyes. Markham softened.

"Okay . . ." Markham turned to the door. "I believe y—"

A bull snorted.

Hair shivered upwards on the back of Markham's neck. The grated staircase clanged with a deafening clamor.

Markham, Yastley, and Gavial turned.

There stood one of the bipedal bull-men from Kloff's turf. Ripped jeans and vest over its bulging grey muscles. Hoof scraping at the floor. It held its enormous machine gun in front of it, and its eyes glowed red.

The bottle on the machine gun began to turn.

Yastley tore open the sauna door. He grabbed Markham and Gavial.

"NO!" said Markham. "YASTLEY, NO!"

Yastley shoved Markham and Gavial into the sauna. Markham hit the moist tile floor, light from the hall slicing over his clothes in dramatic tones.

"NO!" Markham sobbed.

Yastley shoved closed the sauna door.

Through the porthole window, Yastley locked eyes with Markham and saluted.

Bullets spurted from the machine gun and blood splattered the window.

THIRTY-TWO

"God," Markham choked.

Gavial pulled him off the floor. The bull took a few booming steps closer to the door and then—*Pop! Pop!*

It let out a strangled honking noise and thundered to the ground. Someone passing by must have shot it in the head with a pistol. Seconds too late.

Markham caught air in gasps. Gavial's claws squeezed him.

He served you. He died happy.

Markham nodded, but it felt like a watermelon was in his throat.

That's when he remembered why Yastley had led him here. Markham and Gavial both turned to the sauna.

Nothing had changed position. Opaque white orbs still illuminated beneath the rim of the hot pool. The brown seaweed-tangled aquarium made up either wall on the left and right. Swim trunks lined the shelf next to the marble-columned bust of a bearded sea king, and the water heater knob flashed the pool's temperature on the opposite wall. The long, large bath was murky and dark like a dirty smock. It lapped against itself with a little extra personality due to the trembling of the ship. The smell of chlorine filled Markham's nose, and a delicate, single dripping sound reverberated against the tile like a leaky sink.

No one was there. No dark figures lurked around the rim of the pool. Steam rose to hide no one.

Except . . .

Markham stepped forward to the edge of the bath.

Across from him, almost a hundred yards away, someone waded at the end of the pool. Brown clothes billowed around him in the water, and he stared ahead (presumably) with blue sunglasses on. An impossibly long grey beard trickled into the water and extended all the way to just a few feet from the tips of Markham's black shoes. Bubbles pattered in the water all around him.

The figure was unmoving. The figure was silent.

Markham exchanged a look with Gavial. They shared the same sentiment. *Who else could it be?*

Markham looked back at the vague bather. He drew in breath.

"Obensteen." Markham's call rebounded.

Suddenly the seething bubbles in the pool stopped.

Silence fell over them. Gavial hummed an anticipatory little note.

"I'm . . . uh." Markham cleared his throat. "I am Captain Brody." His voice rang. "Your former apprentice Kloff has partnered with your nemesis, Babsy, and together they are taking over my ship."

Still the bather was unmoving. Still the bather was silent.

"If your men would join me," said Markham. "I would grant you—"

Markham stopped. A ticking noise echoed through the ceiling. He raised and narrowed his eyes to it.

The ticking continued, slowly . . .

What's wrong? said Gavial.

"*Shh* . . ." Markham put up a hand.

Now, over by the very vent from which Crocidius' claw had fallen, laughter resonated.

"Down you go . . ."

A slim, shadowed figure lowered through the vent and landed on the floor. Markham gagged in shock and slapped to the ground on his stomach to keep hidden.

Nina, with duct tape confining her hands, feet, and mouth, scurried on her back away from the vent opening above her, buzzing unintelligibly into the tape. Rolls of yellow fat slinked down from the vent next, and Kloff splat down onto the tile, jiggling like a plate of lemon gelatin.

He was aiming Lil' Tucuxi at her, pressing the dorsal fin and sending live footage to the Silly Studio.

"This is better," said Kloff. "Nice and quiet and away from aaaaaanybody. Where is our sweet Captain?" He thumped towards Nina as she continued to crawl backwards. Trickles of lava dripped down his body and glowed. He was still feeding out signals with the nose of the miniature dolphin. "Not here to save you? How about that oversized iguana? Is he—?"

Crack! Crack!

Kloff's eyes popped wide, and he twirled his head to the ceiling, to the vent he'd just come from. The hidden pipes above seemed to crackle and break like ice shattering on a frozen pond . . .

Then—

BOOM!

Crocidius burst through the ceiling and onto the ground on all four limbs. His body was curved and poised for attack, his eyes soulless. Jaw open and oozing slime. Nearly fifteen feet long including his tail.

Smoke blasted from Kloff's mouth as he dropped Lil' Tucuxi and it broke. He retreated a few steps and fell with an enormous rumble onto his back.

Markham bolted to his feet and ran for Nina while Kloff was distracted. He dove his arms under her shoulders and legs and lifted her, standing.

She buzzed muffled sounds of happiness and relief. Markham hushed her lovingly and held her up to Gavial, who scissored the silver duct tape with his claws.

"N-No," said Kloff, as Crocidius closed in. "It's not what you think!" said Kloff. "I wouldn'ta touched her! We—We go way back, Crocidy, we—"

Crocidius lunged for Kloff. He pierced his jaw into the folds of fat that made up the mob lord and flipped up his powerful head. In one colossal move of strength, Crocidius stood and pushed his claw into Kloff's body and lifted him up over his head. He roared. Spit and blood sprayed from his mouth everywhere.

The claw sank into flesh. Kloff howled in pain.

Markham set Nina on her feet and shielded her with an arm across her chest, coursing them both backwards with Gavial at their side. He pushed her under the cover of a bench at the wall and crouched next to her.

Then, just as Crocidius' long jaw reached up to close Kloff's neck between it, the lights in the sauna cut to black.

Markham couldn't see an inch past his nose.

The only sounds were the water splashing back and forth in the pool and the confused clucking of Gavial. Even Crocidius and Kloff seemed to have frozen.

Over in the direction of where the door should be, two long sticks of red glowed and floated in the blackness.

The eyes blinked.

THIRTY-THREE

"Wake up, wake up, wake up, Obensteen . . ." said Babsy. His whiskers twitched audibly, and he chuckled. His legs clicked into the room over the tile. Two pairs of feet on either side of him—webbed-toed—dragged slithering chains and seaweed behind them. They wore huge brass helmets and blubbered out bubbles inside of them like scuba divers. They must have been Babsy's guard, but Markham couldn't see anything more than shapes. All was still black.

Markham's breath seemed ten times louder in his ears. He watched the glow of Babsy's eyes move as the crab's five skeletal legs crawled around the edge of the bath. Babsy's voice was harsh, as if salt had crystallized in his throat after all those years clinging to the outside of the ship.

"Do you remember . . . *we* used to rule this ship . . ."

Gavial hummed in discomfort, as if he remembered indeed.

"They say you *were* the ocean . . . and with me . . . we brought them here from the deepest trenches . . ."

He kept prowling, still addressing Obensteen.

"Now your young comes to me . . . asking what I saw in the deep open blue . . . shouldn't they all know?"

Babsy stopped. His eyes blinked, one at a time.

"*We were the gods.*"

Silence.

"AND NOW YOU HIDE!"

A huge quantity of water splashed against the side of the bath.

Something rose out of the pool.

Babsy's eyes dilated. They shot left to right. His voice was now touched with fear. "You allowed a weak, *soft-shell* Captain to sentence me to prison and turn you into a petty fugitive. We were going to . . . to . . ."

Water streamed off clothing and onto the floor just behind Babsy. Babsy's eyes started to turn around with him.

A bearded mouth dipped into the red glow of Babsy's eyes. It spoke into his ear.

"Boo."

Babsy's eyes and legs zipped into his shell. He clunked onto the floor and could be heard rolling away.

Obensteen gave a deep, hearty laugh.

"It's really him," Markham breathed.

"Obensteeeeen!!!" That was Kloff. He wept. "I'm sorry, Obensteen! I'll never go off and form my own gang ever again!"

Babsy chinked back out of his shell like a cash register popping open.

"Help me, Obensteen!" said Kloff. "I'll never—"

"HUSH, JUNIOR!" Babsy rasped.

"You took this too far, Babsy . . ." Obensteen's voice was a few paces away from where it had once been. It was deep and measured, the way one closes an ancient door slowly so as not to wake the house.

"You didn't take it far enough!" Babsy hissed. "You *ruled the underwater city!* Now you rule slot machines!"

"We are no gods on *Makohoni's* ship . . ." said Obensteen.

"Obensteeeeeen!" Kloff wailed. Crocidius' claw must have been digging in deeper and deeper.

"SHUT UP!" said Babsy, with the sound of a flare gun cocking in his grasp. Obensteen's tall, shadowed figure shoved Babsy's aim away from Kloff.

The flare gun fired in the direction of Markham instead.

The flare crashed into the bench and exploded in hundreds of sparks that trailed and whizzed along the tile, lighting up the sheen of moisture in the room like a firecracker.

Markham fell onto the floor in the open. His Captain's hat in place, jacket, buttons, amulet . . .

Babsy's eyes widened at the sight of Markham. His voice was like an ice machine.

"He's here!"

He raised his gun again and scurried forward.

Bam!

The flare hurtled at Markham and hit him in the chest. Before it exploded, Gavial jumped on Markham and rolled him into the pool. They bowled deep into the water with a crash and a swish of bubbles and foam. The flare fizzled out immediately.

Markham pumped himself as hard as he could for the surface. As soon as he broke into air, eyes still closed, he shouted.

"GO!"

With that cry, several things happened at once: Crocidius roared and tore off Kloff's head. He hurled it at one of Babsy's mobsters and let Kloff's giant body fall to the ground. Babsy plunged into the pool after Gavial, and the two latched together and thrashed around in the water like a great white shark caught on a metal cage.

Markham swam hard to the edge of the rolling bath and leapt out of it. Nina's hands were there, guiding him through the darkness away from the pool. Babsy's second guard charged for Obensteen—or, in the direction he'd last heard his voice. By the sound of a large body smacking into another, he'd found his target.

Crocidius snarled and took down the other guard, whipping his teeth back and forth over his chest.

"Who do we help first?!" said Nina.

"No one," Markham breathed. He pushed her back and loped for the other side of the pool, opposite where Gavial fought with Babsy. "*They help me.*"

Markham's hands explored the wall rapidly in the dark.

"What are you doing?!" said Nina. Without knowing the answer, she lent her hands to search along the wall, too.

"The water heater," said Markham. "It's somewhere on this— *Ha!*"

He found it. But before he could do anything, water burst from the bath and a huge figure crashed into the wall near the destroyed bench. Water cascaded down in large slogs.

"That was Gavial," said Markham. "Go help him. Babsy only wants one man."

Nina disappeared from his side into the darkness where Gavial had crashed.

Markham's hand found the knob, and he jacked it to the left, into deepest red. "Let's boil this crab," he said.

The pool began to bubble and heat.

"HEY. BABSY!"

Those crab legs clacked over the rim of the bath and onto the tile. Babsy's red eyes turned in the direction of Markham's voice. They landed right on his silhouette and narrowed.

"I'M THE GOD YOU WANT!" Markham shouted into the sauna. His voice bounced off the walls. "IT'S ME!"

"*Markham!*" Nina yelled from the corner. He kept his gaze on Babsy, who bounded to him at his invitation.

"*You will be god no more, Captain Brodyyy!*" Babsy fumed. He thrust his spear-like leg at Markham's head. Markham dodged. He grabbed Babsy's glowing eyes and yanked them towards him. Babsy squealed and blinked, legs scampering backwards in panic.

"COME ON!" Markham shouted. Backing up farther.

Leading Babsy away from Nina and Gavial.

Markham ducked as Babsy slashed with a pincer. Another appendage swung down at Markham and pierced his thick coat, scraping down his skin. Markham sucked in breath. He backed up farther and staggered into a shelf of swim trunks.

They flumped to the ground around him. He spun and grabbed a pair of trunks. Just as another leg was about to pierce into his side, Markham pulled the trunks over Babsy's eyes. They glowed like a lampshade, and Babsy's legs splayed for a moment before he regained himself.

Markham held fast to the swim trunks and leaned forward.

"*Boo.*"

Babsy jerked all his limbs into his shell as he did before. His barnacle-ridden shell clunked to the floor.

Markham grabbed Babsy's flare gun. He cocked it directly into an orifice in Babsy's shell.

STOP YOU FOOL! Crocidius yelled. *IT'LL BLAST EVERYWHERE!*

"I know," said Markham. He closed his eyes and pulled the trigger.

BAM!

The firecracker shot into Babsy's shell. Markham jumped onto Babsy and covered the holes with his body. Eyes clenched tight.

Babsy squirmed in panic in his shell, jolting over and over with Markham until—

An explosion of light and fire blew from Babsy's shell.

White flashed into Markham's vision. He fell off Babsy, and his hearing shifted to a shrill, sharp ring.

Babsy screamed in pain in his shell, the sound of fire licking off his legs and his barnacled back. He rolled for the relief of the bath, farther . . . farther . . .

SPLASH!

Babsy plunged into the pool and was met with a deafening sizzle.

THIRTY-FOUR

Crocidius looked down at Markham.

Markham blinked away the fuzz of purple and pink in his sight. The lights were back on in the sauna, brighter than ever before—or so it seemed in his head. He breathed unevenly, and every intake hurt his lungs.

You survived, said Crocidius. His black eyes flashed and didn't seem too excited about it.

"H . . . How?" Markham coughed.

Shirt . . . said Crocidius.

Markham looked down at his chest. His mouth sank open.

Beneath the Captain's uniform was his fiery-patterned volcano shirt. He'd forgotten. The ashy smell of singed cotton and burnt flesh still intoxicated his nostrils. On one foot, he could see his black sock protruding out of the sole of his shoe.

You forgot it was on you? said Crocidius. *You thought you would die killing Babsy for us?*

Markham paused. Nodded.

A beat of begrudging respect from Crocidius followed.

Crocidius reached down his one whole hand for Markham. Markham grabbed it and rose. He swayed.

"Babsy?"

Boiled.

Markham looked into the water. Babsy was illuminated in the forked, webbing light underneath the pool, legs bright red.

Babsy's large, webbed-toed guards had been mauled apart and now lay on the floor, no longer a threat. But Markham jumped when he looked in the direction of Nina.

Obensteen stood next to her, sunglasses still on above his sickeningly long grey beard. His draping brown clothes blocked from view whatever he was looking down at. Nina was beside him on her knees, her back facing Markham.

Hush, said Crocidius. Annoyed. *Obensteen sent his men for you. They are running off the last of the prisoners.*

Markham's mouth hung open.

"W-Why? I didn't offer him anything."

Crocidius snarled. He shoved Markham towards Nina.

Say your goodbyes.

"What?"

Another snarl. Crocidius turned away.

In a daze, Markham moved forward. And here, closer, he could hear Nina's sobs. Obensteen turned wordlessly to Markham as he approached, and then stepped backwards, allowing him space. Markham's eyes fell to the point of interest on the floor.

Gavial.

Punctures from Babsy's pincers riddled his bright green body. Milk clouded his eyes. His toothless jaw was closed, and his head rested on Nina's lap. She stroked him and shook with sorrow.

Markham fell to his knees. He laid his hand over the rough green scales of Gavial.

"He . . ."

"Gavial," said Nina in a tiny voice. She continued to stroke him, tears clinging to her delicate lashes. Her face was flushed.

Gavial hummed. He looked forward, muscles tight with pain, and approaching death making his eyes paler and paler.

Watch over my young, said Gavial.

"I will," said Nina, her voice thick and muffled. Markham crept an arm around her shoulders.

No, Nina, said Gavial. *I spoke to Markham.* A loving beat.

My young is you.

Gavial shuddered in Nina's arms, and then . . . his great body became still, and his eyes slipped entirely into whiteness.

Nina collapsed over him and cried into his bumpy skin. A pulse throbbed in Markham's throat. He tossed a glance at Crocidius, who stood on both legs in the corner of the sauna, watching darkly.

And then Markham turned his eyes to Obensteen above them.

Obensteen tilted his head down at Markham, eyes still hidden behind the jazzy shades.

Markham almost spoke. Almost asked Obensteen why he'd agreed to help him. He glanced at the tsunami amulet hanging from Obensteen's neck, and Nina's words in the elevator came back to him . . .

There was no note, and the pod was only marked with a large wave.

Behind Obensteen was the marble bust Markham had seen before. The bust was bearded, eyes blank, a crown of waves on his head . . .

Markham looked at the bust and then again at Obensteen, who stared back at him and allowed the wordlessness to stretch.

The blue of his sunglasses seemed to go on forever.

THIRTY-FIVE

"For almost total annihilation," said Markham, "this ship cleans up well in two weeks."

He took Nina's hands in his own strong ones and applied pressure to her fingers—lovingly massaging the empty space where one of her fingers was missing.

Nina blushed and gave a little smile. She wore a white hibiscus in her hair and a brown sundress with sandals and brown-painted toenails. One of Gavial's nails hung from her neck, next to her sand dollar amulet. "So do you."

Markham grinned crookedly. He stood across from her in full uniform, tall and powerful and handsome as never before. His blue eyes blazed with life, and his silver hair was roguishly mussed. Stubble grazed his face and made him look not older, but more alive and virile. *I guess I am a stubble guy, after all,* he thought. His black dress shoes were whole again and shone like his gold buttons and stripes.

Waterfalls cascaded gently around Markham and Nina from the upper balconies and into the grand pool at the bottom of the atrium. Water lapped against the cream-colored marble island they stood upon.

After Obensteen's cronies aided the passengers and ran off the remains of Kloff and Babsy, the Blue Star Line rejoiced in the victory of their Captain. Panels of the best thinkers, architects, lawyers, and artists offered Markham their service. Together, they decided several things.

First, Obensteen's men would be paid thrice their current salaries to become Mariners and reestablish the department. In return, Obensteen would be named sole Chief Executive Officer of the casinos and retain tax-exempt profits.

Next, prisoners would no longer be biogenetically altered and sent to live outside the ship—the Blue Star Line would construct prisons inside, focused on rehabilitation and community service. No further opportunity for mutinies to foster in the open ocean. Unfortunately, however, those of Babsy's gang had either all died or fled into the mysteries of the dark ocean, far, far away from the ship, rather than accepting any such reintegration.

On all decks every locked cabin in the residence halls was opened, and Deck 58 was swept of all debris and ash. Mops were slapped onto the front steps of 58's courthouse, and in other government buildings, windows and walls were sanded clean. The barricades at the elevator landing and stairwells were torn apart.

They would seek new officers to fill the arched gold buildings soon.

Regarding the death of their beloved Master Gavial, Markham agreed with the panel: The former galley of the ship, now flooded with saltwater from the hole the architects only recently patched up, would be transformed into an indoor lagoon dedicated to Gavial, and the kitchens relocated to Kloff's former territory, in the slums Markham had traveled through, attracting restaurants and jobs for twice as many servers and cooks. That area which had once looked like a rat colony riddled with holes made for a spectacular variety of walk-up food and frozen custard burrows, especially for the passengers with flight or wall-climbing ability.

As for the Kloffers . . .

By going through many documents in his Captain's Quarters, Markham discovered at last why he had seen a strange carving of a Kloffer on the door of the boiler room with the black frogs. Perhaps also why the little black frogs had union concerns.

Many years ago, Kloffers and black frogs worked side-by-side. It made sense, after all . . . Markham recalled that enormous (mother?) volcano in the boiler room.

Any surviving Kloffers willing to switch their allegiance could serve probation and then return to the boilers under the jurisdiction of the frogs. Or, if the Kloffers felt too segregated there, Markham agreed they could also use their volcanic heads to fire up meals in restaurants, pop popcorn in the theater . . . whatever calling of their hearts they felt.

Markham was determined not to repeat any mistake he may have made in his past. He would ensure *all* of his passengers felt ministered to this time.

That lagoon dedicated to Gavial was where Markham and Nina stood now, on that marble island, in the shadow of a twelve-foot-tall statue of Gavial in his chef coat. An urn with Gavial's ashes was cemented at the statue's feet. Next to it wavered a candle, and an eight-by-ten framed photo of the healthy and smiling

First Mate Yastley in his white uniform and silver epaulettes. His silver epaulettes, taken before his cremation, rested at the frame.

White folding chairs surrounded Markham and Nina. In the water of the lagoon, lotus flowers and leis floated.

An audience crowded around the couple, and more beings congested the rails of *every deck* above them, looking down and dropping leis from tens of stories up into the peaceful lagoon below. Reporters and film cameras—Sylvester behind the largest one—focused on Markham and Nina holding hands at the foot of the statue.

That large, bare-chested islander with tan skin and abalone bracelets presided between them, holding *The Captain's Log* to his breast and smiling a rosy, jubilant grin.

He spoke in a native island language that Markham, somehow, understood.

"Friends, the love of Makohoni is showered among us at last, and now flooded to the flower who will soon be his wife."

Tears filled Markham's eyes as he squeezed Nina's hands and smiled at her.

"Here we are further blessed," said the island minister, *"that our Captain, our Eternal Helmsman, the Sacred Skipper, will preside as Admiral forev—"*

Markham dropped his head and held up a hand.

The islander minister stopped. Nina cocked her head at Markham's gesture, nervous. She ran her thumb over his vein on the hand she still held.

Slowly, Markham lifted his other hand to his head. He removed the Captain's hat. The gold anchor at the front and leaves dancing along the black visor flashed in the light of the restored chandelier overhead.

"My . . . treasured passengers," said Markham. He held his hat and stared down at it. Everyone was silent. "I will be your Captain . . ."

He looked up and met Nina's eyes.

"Until the day I die."

Gasps. Some rose from their seats. Passengers turned to one another with worried murmurs. The minister's face was swirled with distress, looking from Markham to Nina and back again.

"The end of the prophecy on the door of the boiler room," said Markham, still looking at Nina. He pushed a half smile onto his face. "I never read you the rest."

He recited it.

"Makohoni is god incarnate, destined to take the form of a Captain. Immortal, but slayable, he shall attract the creations to his service.

"His power, his immortality, so holds as long as his flesh touches no open ocean."

Markham remembered that feeling of a thunderclap when his body hit the ocean surface.

"In many ways the water shall harm him, but his power and immortality shall slowly return if only he grasps the wheel of his ship once more."

Everyone watched and listened, breathless, to the Captain before them.

"But the one I've fallen in love with," Markham finished, closing his eyes painfully, "is the open ocean itself."

"What?" Nina choked, loud enough for only him. Markham gave her a sad purse of his lips back.

But Nina seemed to remember—her expression paled. The reason she'd always been drawn to that endless blue, the poster over her bed, the dreams she had . . .

Her coming from the pod, almost like the ocean presenting its offspring.

"As long as I love you," whispered Markham, "I can't be immortal."

The gathered passengers were dead quiet. Markham pursed his lips again and glanced out at them with bittersweet humor.

"Are you getting all this, Sylvester?"

Passengers turned to look over their shoulders at Sylvester, who was bent behind a long purple camera. He stuck out a thumbs-up. A thundering sound followed as all the passengers turned in their seats back to Markham. While still uncomfortable, a little understanding lightened their sad eyes.

Markham raised his voice for all to hear.

"I will be your Captain until the day I die."

"Markham . . ." Nina's voice pled. She gaped at him as if to say, *I'm not worth it.*

Markham only squeezed her and stepped closer, so that her head almost touched his chest. "But I choose to die with her."

He looked at Nina, though he spoke to the ship at large.

"If I didn't choose to love like you, die like you . . ." Markham replaced the hat back over his head. "What kind of Captain would I be?"

Another long beat of silence.

And then someone in the crowd screamed joyful praise. Others cheered.

Markham grinned and slid Nina's gold and opal-inlaid ring onto the ring finger of the hand that still had one. The band waved like the movement of the ocean.

He leaned in and pressed his lips against hers. The ship shouted approval. Markham engulfed Nina into his thick Captain's coat and dug his mouth into hers harder, feeling all that familiar hot blood jerk through his body. He bowed forward unexpectedly and dipped her. Louder cheers.

When Markham swung back up, holding Nina to his chest, he beamed at her. But the smile flickered off his face as he shifted his gaze over her shoulder, and he groaned.

Thousands of black frogs blackened the marble island.

"Of course," said Markham. Nina laughed.

And then Markham caught sight of something else. Something tall and brown and ghoulish.

Crocidius stood in the shadow of the deck one story up, next to the wall of the elevator. Watching. His face was a scowl. Three bright green baby crocodiles perched blankly on his powerful shoulders.

His reptilian eyes blinked once. There might have been tears in them. Markham's lips rolled into a tight line.

Without thinking, he broke apart from Nina. He stepped aside and faced the audience, raising both hands.

Again, instantly, everyone hushed.

Markham stood there in the silence for a moment. He looked up at Crocidius. The brown crocodile's eyes narrowed, and he shifted in the shadow.

"We lost a good man," said Markham, "in First Mate Yastley. He gave his life for me. And now that position is mournfully empty."

Passengers nodded in heavy, grieved silence.

Markham walked slowly over to Yastley's urn. He crouched down and gathered the silver epaulettes into his hand. Looked down at them. Then, still crouching, he raised his eyes again to Crocidius. He held his gaze there so steadily that others began to follow it. Crocidius' expression shifted to tentative understanding.

"I'd like to announce the new First Mate now."

Excited chatter rose.

Markham rose and extended his free hand, palm upward. "Crocidius."

Eyebrows jumped. Cameras swiveled and flashed up in the direction of Crocidius.

"Would you please come forth?"

Crocidius hesitated in the darkness while Markham stood there, patient and confident.

Slowly, nervously almost, Crocidius' statuesque figure thawed. He moved from the rail.

Like a lizard, bathed in the flash of many cameras, Crocidius crawled on all fours down the deck and into the lagoon. He darted his eyes uncertainly at those watching him as he swam through the water to the island, using his tail as a rudder.

Water splashed and streamed down in a patter as Crocidius mounted the rim.

At last he towered over Markham, water dripping down his brown, swampy skin.

Markham bent his head back and looked up at him.

Palm open, Markham held out the silver epaulettes and offered them to Crocidius.

There was a long pause. Crocidius' teeth twisted down from his closed jaw as he turned his head towards Nina. Nina watched him with love and pride, a little sadness lingering deep beneath there as well.

Markham nodded and spoke so only Crocidius could hear.

"You're more than a First Mate," said Markham. "You're my brother."

Crocidius emitted a low, conflicted growl. His black, vertical pupils stared deep into Markham.

And then, with his one claw, he scraped the epaulettes into his grasp.

The audience cheered louder than ever before, and bulbs cracked while Sylvester hollered for more film. Gavial's three little hatchlings scurried under seats and feet and leapt onto Nina and nuzzled into her hair. Nina laughed.

Markham grabbed Crocidius' arm. He raised their joined hands together over their heads. Crocidius' expression stayed dark and gloomy as he glared around at the ship.

The crystal eye of the statue of Gavial above seemed to twinkle.

Markham straightened the framed photograph of Crocidius— long face grim as ever and shoulders under silver epaulettes— next to Yastley's on the wall of First Mates outside the Captain's Quarters. Markham held an opened Corona Extra in his right hand, his eyes glassy, an easy smile on his face as he gazed at the photo.

It had taken days of convincing for Nina to accept Markham's decision to become mortal for her. But the conversation ended with the swig of a drink much like the one Markham held now. "Maybe we'll look into changing the rules, anyway." He'd hiccupped. "I'm the goddamn Captain."

Nina snuck up behind him now and tugged his body to her by a lapel of the Captain's coat.

"I miss your Hawaiian shirts," she mumbled against his stubble, kissing him. "It's still our honeymoon you know . . ." Her nine fingers fished into his silver hair.

"Ohhh . . ." Markham growled. He moved himself against her and attempted to talk dirty. "I'm gonna . . . uh . . ."

Nina twitched her eyes closed in annoyance. "Don't."

"No, I won't," agreed Markham. "How about we just—"

A heavy tread upset their conversation. Markham took Nina's hand instead and turned towards the sound.

Crocidius, on all fours, turned the corner and crawled up to them. He rose to his feet before Markham.

You need to come to the crow's nest, said Crocidius. *There's something you'll want to see.*

Markham and Nina looked at each other.

Moments later, Markham banged open the ceiling hatch and climbed up from the ladder. Nina and Crocidius close behind.

Cool air met him. The sky glimmered with stars, silver against navy blue, like a mix between the Captain's and First Mate's colors. Somewhere far ahead was the steady sound of the bow bowling aside waves as it cut forward. That constant rhythm of the moving sea was familiar to Markham on deeper levels than he could identify.

On this private wooden crow's nest, high above the gigantic cruise ship, two stone-carved tikis stood sentinel next to an enormous brass telescope. One tiki stared out portside, the other starboard. They wore red goggles so as not to destroy their night vision—if indeed they were living—and so that red and green buoys wouldn't seem closer at night the way they normally would. One of the stone guards seemed to vibrate on the ground as Markham brushed beside it, and he looked down, heart thumping.

The Captain's steering wheel with long mahogany spokes was just ahead of Markham.

Even this high up, the parameters of the ship were indiscernible. Behind, albatross glided in the wake of the ship. Wind whistled through the air currents and tried to lift Markham's hat. A few times, the wind's howl sounded almost human.

Careful . . . Crocidius thrummed. *Sea wind carries many frequencies . . .*

Markham looked at him.

You may hear screams, said Crocidius.

Markham continued to secure Crocidius in his gaze. He took a swig of the Corona.

Crocidius pointed a claw at the telescope.

Markham wiped a hand across his mouth and frowned. He paused for a long beat and then dipped his eye into the lens.

The horizon zoomed into view. Grey water jumping up and down with the minuscule movement of his breathing, and something else . . .

He studied it for several long beats. And then he pulled out.

Markham turned to Nina and Crocidius. Blank.

His eyebrows rose.

"Land ho."

THE END

ACKNOWLEDGEMENTS

Thank you to my family—Kelley, Mom, Dad, and dogs. Thank you particularly to Mom for making the baked goods that celebrated this book's completion so long ago. It really is an "Overboard success!" now.

My agent, Jessica Sinsheimer, continues to be an irreplaceable heroine whose kindness, wisdom, and friendship warms the heart of this ill-behaved client. I thank her and Context Literary for guiding me through the practical details of this book.

I thank and acknowledge my beta readers, Martin Wilsey, Shelley Shearer, Kimberly Ray, Emma G. Rose, Stef Kasko, William Zanotti, Nick Bruner, Tom Ligon, David Keener, and others from the Hourlings and the Writers of Chantilly writing groups.

I hope my charitable buddies, Oceanic Global and Clean Ocean Foundation, will also accept my appreciation.

Many thanks to Tara Rayers, who did a fantastic job copyediting this book (and lobbing me cookies, as requested).

Sara Williams brought a gorgeous front and back cover—with all its enchanting lights—to life, and I am grateful for that.

John H. Matthews lent me his expertise in publication and interior formatting. Love you, John.

Thanks to Seth Trumbo for taking care of my saltwater aquarium, and to my fish for delighting and inspiring me.

Shannon Bairett—thanks for the fan art. I still have it.

I most especially thank the Scribes of Eldion, my dear writing group, which includes Udy Kumra, Tom Pollard, and Katie Kelly. They offered valuable feedback and adopted this weird little book as their own. Prosperity upon Eldion!

Pop, my grandfather, passed away just before the publication of this book. I want the world to know I loved him. (Joseph Megale, 1929-2023).

As always, I leave the final acknowledgement to Matt. My big brother. He and I enjoyed cruising the Caribbean and rejecting all the beautiful cuisine in favor of "Inky's Treasure," which was the kid's menu name for chicken tenders and fries. We had it every night.

I miss him.

Thanks for seeing a Captain in me.

ABOUT THE AUTHOR

S.C. Megale—or Shea—is a traditionally-published author and adventurer. An American born in 1995, Megale was diagnosed with a rare form of muscular dystrophy and has defied odds ever since—meeting the Pope, shadowing Hollywood film sets, diving the Great Barrier Reef, receiving a fraternal knighthood, and walking through Stonehenge. Megale authored *This is Not a Love Scene* (St. Martin's Press, 2019), *American Boy* (Bluebullseye Press, 2019, and first-place IPPY Award and Reader Views Literary Award winner), and *Hockey's Hidden Gods* (Rowman & Littlefield, 2022).

Megale serves in the United States Coast Guard Auxiliary and is a certified Master Naturalist. The author graduated with distinction from the University of Virginia with a major in history, a minor in astronomy, and a language proficiency in American Sign Language (ASL), and currently studies as a master's student at Georgetown University.

Most fittingly for this work, Megale loves the ocean, wildlife, and dogs—and almost exclusively wears Hawaiian shirts.

For more information—or if you simply need a friend whose hand to hold—please visit www.scmegale.com.

MORE FROM S.C. MEGALE

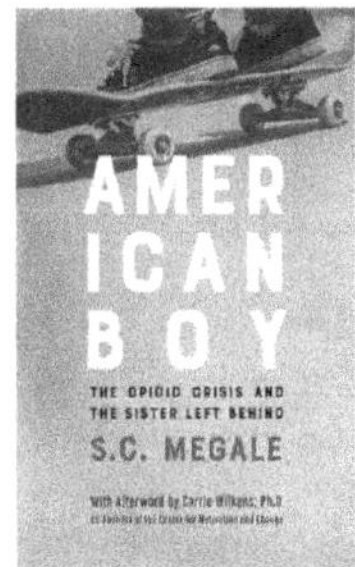

If you enjoyed *Overboard*, please leave a review on Goodreads and Amazon, Barnes & Noble, or wherever you made your purchase. It really helps!

Thank you.